HELL FIRE

Jack Moskovitz

RAMBLE HOUSE

ISBN 13: 978-1-60543-331-8

ISBN 10: 1-60543-331-4

Cover Art: Gavin L. O'Keefe
Preparation: Fender Tucker

To my gal-pal, Johnnie Mae Hawkins who likes
kittens, thrift shopping, her newest great
granddaughters, and me. Twelve years
we have been living our marriage
under God. I pray for
twelve more.

Bathos from the Fires of Hell

Introduction by Fender Tucker, Publisher

In late June of 2009 I received a letter (with SASE) from a Jack Moskovitz of Omaha NE asking me if I'd be interested in publishing his new hardboiled novel, HELL FIRE. It was typed on an old (I think) typewriter and as unusual as that was, the book itself was even more surprising. But first, here's Jack's description of himself.

An elderly bachelor languishes in the Midwest. His name is Jack Moskovitz. He's a retired civil servant who, in search of honest part-time employment, has washed dishes and bused tables in steakhouses, been a radio DJ, sold magazine subs over the phone. For the past sixty-five years he has authored soft core porn novels, poems, short stories, literary novels, hardboiled crime, stage plays for adults and children. Two audio plays are awaiting production by San Francisco's Shoestring Audio Theater.

In the late sixties-early seventies he sold 45,000-worders to Corinth in San Diego, American Art in Los Angeles and Bee-line Books, NYC. A G-rated one act is available from Lazy Bee Scripts. Two works of narrative fiction may be viewed at Kingfisher Books on the web. During the eighties Moscovitz was active in the mail art movement. This is the first of his thrillers published by Ramble House.

Great! Here was one of those guys I read about in SIN-A-RAMA, a writer who risked going to jail for pressing a forbidden sequence of keys.

I was also intrigued by the typewriter, since it reminded me of the manuscripts of Harry Stephen Keeler's that were loaned to me years back by Francis M. Nevins. Typewritten manuscripts are quaint, nostalgic and sincere, but most of all, they are extreme bitches to OCR and edit. But Jack said that even if I didn't find the story publishable, I'd still have a hell of a read. He was right.

My first thought as I read and edited the badly OCRed text was: Remember all those stories you read or see on TV and in the movies where they simply ignore the fact that human beings generally excrete a few times a day? Stories whose plots would be drastically different if the author had to explain how the two Hollywood hostages maintained their splendid coifs and pristine pants, even though they were tied back to back for three days? Talk about too much, too soon!

Well, Jack makes up for those wimpy plots with a vengeance. He pulls no punches and he even throws in a bladder problem that had me cringing with every descriptive sentence. Yow! This is really scary! I'm sorry, but the most dreadful word in the English language has to be the word "catheter".

But what really impressed me about Jack's writing was his all-out attack on pronouns. Obviously he's not getting paid by the word because he leaves out practically every opening pronoun he can. Makes the action move real fast. Can't put the book down. Gotta get to the next paragraph.

I imagine if Jack had sent this to a major publisher they would have wanted him to beef it up to 400 pages and get into the details of that catheter thing, but I like this story just the way it is. It reminds me of the guitars in the early Beatle songs: raw, brash, a little bit arrogant. And most of all, authentic.

I look forward to more of Jack Moskovitz's novels. Read on and I think you'll want more, too.

KRAGER, SMITH AND MILLER did not know they were being watched.

Four blocks from their target they unloaded the van.

Four A.M.

The sharp November wind drove the mist against their flame-resistant body armor. A homeless man, too drunk to care, slumped against the first alley entrance they passed.

Already the security guards checked the double locks on the Manvitz Jewelry Brokerage House double doors.

Krager, Smith and Miller zipped their flame resistant suits, waited in alley shadows a half block away. At the other end of the alley a forty watt night light over a steel door, sheathed the door, top to bottom, but couldn't illuminate the gaps in the adjoining bricks.

The security guards drove off. The trio lugged their gear to the jewelry company's front door.

On the warehouse roof directly overhead Carl Dorn, the retired arson cop, watched.

Krager stuck an oblong pouch midway across the front door. He uncoiled leader wires across the sidewalk, into the intersection where Smith and Miller waited.

The traffic signal above them changed color. Behind their target a homeless man searched a dumpster.

Krager punched the detonator button.

Double paned doors and adjoining windows shattered. Splintered glass, twisting steel frames, the whoosh of flames advancing inside the building toward the rear office made high-pitched obscene noises.

They put on their hoods.

Ignoring the destroyed display cases and the exposed pieces, the trio ran the aisle to a smoldering oak door. Miller wielded a hammer. They climbed over the shards and into the office.

A late model Stoolshoes Security wall safe, across the room, was next to a large oak desk. The safe door was six inches thick.

Krager taped a small oblong pouch across the door.

Outside, two security guards, unable to bridge the flames, fired their weapons from the curb. As he crossed the office Kramer pulled a rocket launcher from the sheath attached to his right shoulder.

The concussion missile pierced floor to ceiling flame, hitting the guard nearest the entrance. He and his partner, weapons flying, flailed, exploded.

Krager's joyful scream was muffled by cracking plaster, wood support beams.

An instant's pause while he enjoyed the carnage he had created. Then he and the other two pulled the desk past the office entrance, into what remained of the showroom.

They crouched. The desk was between them and the safe.

Krager activated the detonator. The safe door flew off its hinges.

The trio filled thirty gallon asbestos-lined bags with the contents.

Krager placed the grapefruit-sized Hell Fire ruby in his hip pouch.

They fled through the store, to the street, to the van's rear doors.

Four blocks away sirens screamed.

Carl Dorn came up behind Miller and Smith, fired twice, then ducked. Steel jackets punctured skull tissue. Miller and Smith slammed against the van door. Brain matter slid to the handles.

Before Miller and Smith slumped to the street, Dorn said to Krager:

"Buy you a beer?"

II

A T SIX A.M. Dorn and Krager sat at Dorn's kitchen table drinking a regional brew. With his retirement bonus Dorn bought this one story white frame bungalow on a midtown Omaha side street.

After forty years of one room efficiency apartments he wanted a bigger place to die in.

He almost died in Dachau. When he was ten his parents and grandparents were given their final showers in a quonset hut that had no water.

Seventy-five now with a prostate riddled with tumors and lungs blackened with ash.

Krager was late forties, solidly built. A warehouse dockman was how he looked. Prolonged exposure to high grade liquid explosives singed his retinas. He wore prescription sunglasses.

On the table between them was a package of blunts. Dorn fired one. Krager did the same. The younger man examined the flame of the lighter in his hand before he shut the lid.

"One thing better than one fire and that's two," Krager said.

"Between a fire and an inferno?"

A grin. "More light from a big one. The world needs more light." He moistened his lips. "More light. More trust, boss."

"I like to watch."

"I'd have paid off Miller and Smith. Don't enjoy it like you do."

"Paying off people like Miller and Smith's my business."

"Your pleasure?"

"You know the answer."

Krager turned toward the dining room shadows.

Dorn cocked his head. "Hear something?"

"The wind, I guess."

"Lot of it this time of the year."

"All that stuff in the dining room is making me jumpy."

"Won't be there very long." Dorn coughed. Beer washed it away.

"Payoff is when?"

"Ten. This morning."

"That next job you mentioned yesterday pays . . ."

"Sure it pays."

"How much?" Krager directed smoke at the water-spotted ceiling.

Dorn named the fee. "Small bills. Plus the work. Lots of it."

"I like the heat like you like the ice. Where's the sin?"

"I iced Miller and his friend because they were skinheads."

"First time I saw them without hats they damn near blinded me. Sunny day."

"I wasn't making a hair style statement, understand."

"American Nazis, weren't they?"

"Swastikas on their wrists gave it away. I took it away. Had to."

"Nobody's perfect." Pat Krager blinked at the ceiling.

The largest water spot was shaped like the Italian "boot" on a world map.

"My share buys a new roof and an inside paint job," Dorn said. "In case I want to sell."

"I'd like to go overseas. Can't get a passport. One more restriction an ex-con lives with."

"Had enough overseas travel when I lived overseas. After Dachau I gave up on Europe. On God."

Krager yawned. "Heard of Him. It."

The arsonist uncoiled himself from the long legged dinette stool. "Wanna leave after the payoff?"

"Ten-oh-five." Dorn walked Krager to the basement landing, and the outside door.

The van was parked in the driveway a few feet away.

"Need to clean the van, pluck a chicken." Kruger tensed, looked down the long flight of stairs into basement shadows.

He laughed. "Thought I heard mice."
"Wind."
Krager turned up his coat collar. "That's what it was."
He went out into pre-dawn darkness.

III

KRAGER MADE a five minute stop at Mae Hogan's, in downtown Omaha. Kittsy, a short, big boned blonde, finished him off fast.

"Can't help but notice," she said.

He zipped his fly. "Notice what?"

"Two big things. Your wallet's the other thing."

"I make a living." He laced his discount house shoes.

"Often as you're here it has to be more than just a living."

"I live on the cheap. Got a room with no view at the Overland over by the rail yards. Save the coins for your loins."

She ignored the rhyme. "I do all nighters. Keep you dancin' and romancin'. Good everything. Including the price."

"This old guy I know. About ready to sell his crib for hospice care, I think. A shot of you might make old age less painful."

"Think I'm old?" She tied the robe sash tight to her plump stomach.

"Him. Not you." He tucked a dollar bill in the exposed cleavage.

He noticed the tattoo under her left breast.

"Bring him over," she said.

"If I think about it." He went out the door and down the hall to the elevator.

She douched at the sink, read the German language newspapers *der Geist der Stets Verneint.*

IV

While Krager was having his ashes hauled at Hogan's, Carl Dorn was on the phone.

"I have it," Dorn said. "Where's Emil Nauman?"

"Withersville, Idaho. Has a compound there. A rally's scheduled there. Don't know when yet. Here's the street address. Ten Eleven Delaware Road. Nauman rides a bed these days. Drop in any time. He'll be home."

"Any others?"

"Between Omaha and Withersville? One ten-member cell in your neighborhood." Another address. "Mayer Pred will be there at ten."

Dorn went to the bathroom, voided a few drops. He washed his hands, washed his penis. After drying, he lubricated a catheter, eased it past the prostate, into the bladder. He voided, wincing when the bladder emptied and the catheter jerked. He washed, then placed the rubber tube on a towel on the bathtub shelf.

The prostate, swollen with tumors, prevented a normal flow. After surgery he would have no trouble urinating. Stopping would be the problem.

He turned on the light above the stove.

"Born to a diaper," he told the coffee pot. "Die in one."

He brewed coffee.

V

S aw something. Maybe nothing down at Hogan's," Krager said at nine thirty.

Dorn re-filled Krager's cup. "What?"

After a sip, the younger man said: "This chubby tummy I bounced off of down there. Name's Kittsy. Swastika's under her left tit. Doubt it's a birth mark."

"Her last name?"

"Don't know. Not even sure her name's Kittsy."

Dorn consulted the list given him over the phone.

"Kittsy Vreeland?" Dorn said.

Krager paused, sipped, said: "Could be."

He wiped his clean shaven upper lip with the three for a dollar washcloth he used for a handkerchief.

"Hate's expensive, ain't it, Carl?"

"The Hell Fire project bought information, plus a small bonus for me and your usual fee."

"Travel time included in this next job?"

"By the mile. Whorehouses and casinos come out of your end. I cover everything else."

A car door slammed. Dorn looked at his watch.

"Right on time." Dorn started for the front door.

VI

MAYER PRED did not introduce himself to Pat Krager. He was eighty, short, thin, bald with a pencil line moustache. His brown suit, like Dorn's, was creaseless, frayed, His gray tie was flecked with souvenirs of too many bowls of soup.

He placed an attaché case on the dining room table, unlocked the security lock, lifted the lid.

The Hell Fire Ruby changed hands.

The thirty gallon bags contents went into a large canvas bag on the floor.

Glancing at Krager, Mayer said in Yiddish: "Never trust another thief."

Dorn said: "Known him since we were on opposite sides. Cut him a break once so he didn't get maximum jail time. Been friends since. He's okay."

"They all are until the jackboots come down. But you know that."

"When's the rally?"

"Finding anyone who knows anything is a slow process. When you reach Withersville we will have the information."

Mayer Pred checked the attaché case's lock. "Well, gentlemen," he said in English. "A pleasure."

After he left and Krager finished counting, Carl said: "Time to go."

Krager tucked the envelope, swollen with bills, in the equipment case on the floor next to his chair. "Crew?"

"Just us."

Dorn's suitcase contained an unlicensed thirty-eight police special, shells, spring loaded shoulder holster, toothbrush, paste for sensitive teeth, dental floss, two underwear changes, and the catheter and lubricant.

He double-checked the dead bolts on the side and front doors, set the timers on the front and bed room lamps, put on a wool-lined rain coat, gloves, two dollar knock-off of a Russian cossack hat with ear flaps.

"Ready for winter, Carl?"

"Or Hell, if it's cold."

Inside the van, Pat said: "Where to, boss?"

VII

ORNING RUSH HOUR traffic over the Nebraska-Iowa Bridge stopped. Started. Stopped.

Horns blared.

Forty degrees and sunny. Puddles filled the sagging macadam surface.

"Sun's brighter than a whore's eyes after a forty dollar tip." Krager reached into the jacket pocket for the sunglasses.

Dorn grunted.

The Missouri River's morning breath infiltrated through the closed wing vents. Untreated sewage competed with the old man's urine and sweat, the unwashed underwear. The brown suit's mothballs odor; it was last cleaned for his wife's funeral eight years ago.

Across the bridge traffic branched out.

Through the Council Bluffs, Iowa west end business district, up a hill, to the one story light blue wood frame house at the crest.

En route, Krager ran his plan.

One house up there. Krager U-turned the van in the gravel road and did it slowly. The occupants might be suspicious of an unfamiliar van with Nebraska plates and Omaha license tags.

He pointed the van down the hill and parked a half block from the target. He left the motor running.

"They'll think we're two blue collar types delivering a package," Krager said.

"We are."

Krager held his package under his arm.

He went up the front steps to the front door. Dorn took the driveway to the open garage door.

The radio blared. Noise vibrated off the garage's cement walls.

The undercarriage of a late model sports utility vehicle was being worked on. Krager stretched the explosive-filled pouch across the front door.

Dorn entered the garage.

The mechanic's feet were visible. A single jack elevated the SUV.

Dorn left the thirty-eight in the holster. He took a deep breath before he pulled the jack. Two thousand pounds crashed to the cement floor.

Then came the blood. Always the blood.

He did a little dance to avoid the flow as the bomb at the front door went off.

VIII

THE ROOF lifted from the barge rafters, disintegrated. Six shingles, all that remained of the roof, fell across the driveway.

Front and rear walls collapsed. Echoes strong enough to wake the dead woke night workers sleeping off their after-work whiskeys, eight blocks away.

Concussions rattled naked elm branches a half mile down the hill.

Dorn fell on his side. The thirty-eight slipped from his damp hand. His sinuses drained. His eyes teared. The vibrations nearly activated his bladder.

The blast's force activated a second heartbeat, strong as the first.

He retched, groped for the thirty-eight.

His ears thrummed, a steady, painful, single, low pitched tone.

Dorn struggled to a crouch. Krager, at his side, hoisted the old man to his feet.

The basement door flew open.

Two middle aged men, bald and bearded, staggered across the cement floor.

From the driveway Dorn fired twice. The men fell, lay still.

A younger man with a Hitler moustache tripped, fell. His clothes were on fire.

Dorn took a single step toward the man.

Sobbing, the Hitler wanna-be lay on his face, struggling with the leather vest curling across his shoulders.

The old man fired twice. Steel jackets tore the back of the man's head.

"Help . . . help me . . ." A female voice from the basement stairs.

Kittsy Vreeland appeared, nude, at the open basement door.

"She's mine, Carl."

Kittsy Vreeland's hair was on fire. Krager carried her to the driveway, to the outside hose, turned the water full force. She screamed. The cold spray doused the flames, washed ash from her broad shoulders. Stiff nippled breasts quivered. belly and thighs spasmed. Skin blushed.

She voided, screamed.

Krager cupped her buttocks, hoisted her, held her against his chest. Her sobs deepened. She retched, trembled.

"Drop her, Pat."

"Not likely. She's the best piece I've had since . . . last week."

She slumped in his arms.

Holding her close, Krager hurried toward the van.

In the street below, people looked.

In the van, the arsonist wrapped her in an old blanket.

Eyelids fluttering, she shrieked.

Krager found a pillow, lowered her head to it.

"First liquor store we come to I'll get you some nerve medicine."

Tears spilled. Her eyes were luminous. The screams ceased.

She hugged herself.

From the passenger's seat, Dorn said: "Pat, she's your problem."

"A fancy woman's no problem." Krager released the hand brake, guided the van down the hill.

IX

HALF HOUR LATER they reached a strip mall outside town.

Krager looked at the sleeping woman, then at Dorn.

"Need anything, Carl?"

"Need to get where we're going," the retired arson cop said.

Krager entered the liquor store. Dorn took the catheter and lube into the outside bathroom.

When they got back in the van, the arsonist dropped a clothing bag on the floor behind the driver's seat. The liquor store purchase went into the slot between the driver's and front passenger's seats. Pat removed the sunglasses, rubbed his eyes.

A station wagon, carrying four white haired women, pulled in, almost striking the van.

Putting on the sun glasses, Krager yelled: "Look out, ladies. Blind man driving."

The women clucked like hens fattening up for Sunday dinner.

Kittsy moaned.

Dorn flinched.

"Okay, boss?"

"Why?"

"You shivered."

"It's November. Why wouldn't I?"

Krager drove onto the highway shoulder.

"Carl, my eyes feel like they're jammed into my skull. Take over?"

Dorn came around to the driver's side. "Give her one for me."

"I'll give her one for me."

She woke up, clutching the blanket. Her breasts quivered. The nipples were irritated by the coverlet's roughness. Sour, vaginal odors raised gooseflesh on the elderly man's thighs. It raised nothing else.

Krager passed the bottle.

Dorn said: "Not before dark."

He passed it to the girl.

She took a sip. "Ah, good shit." Another swallow before she handed it back.

"Don't need it." Krager lip-chewed. "Boss, I think we should stop. Right now. Eat. Give our guest a chance to recover. Like that."

Dorn turned to face her. "Feel like more travel time?"

She blinked. "Got to do . . . you know."

Krager pulled onto a dirt road that bisected an elm copse.

At road's end was a two-story wood frame house, with an open porch. The gray facade was speckled with pigeon droppings. In front of the entrance a rusted metal chair lay on its side. Pigeons roosted on the barge rafters, tapped across bloated shingles, the porch's sagging planks. The "For Sale" sign was buried in the weeds.

"I feel like this dump looks," Dorn said.

"Like a carpenter took a dump and let the waste form its own identity," Krager smiled. "I get poetic when I'm within planting distance of a sweet potato."

"Any ass-wiping paper?" She climbed out.

"Forgot to buy some." Krager patted her rump.

She slapped his hand. "Save the passion for when I'm on the clock."

"Got a copy of last Sunday's Omaha World Herald." He reached over the driver's seat, found the paper on the van floor. "Editorial pages."

He tossed them.

"Ass wipe is what their opinions are worth," Dorn said.

Still blanket-wrapped, she hip-switched into the copse.

"Whore's walk," Pat said. "Parade's the merchandise like a starlet at a producers' convention."

Dorn said: "That white, senile fuck who managed the paper. Most people have acknowledged Israel's right to exist. Except that white, deaf as a turd fuck."

"Yeah, boss, got to watch out for those fuckers."

Breezes stirred the elm's top branches. Otherwise, no activity within the copse.

Breathing hard, Krager got out. "Miss me when I'm gone?"

"Go, and we'll find out." Settled in the seat, Dorn stretched his legs.

"Maybe she fell down a ravine," Krager said, over his shoulder.

"Maybe she's breeding with a mountain lion."

"Takes all kinds to make a hooker's day."

X

KRAGER FOUND HER a few feet into the copse. The blanket, folded at her left foot, attracted one hundred red ants. Urine plunged them into confusion—a scattering tering within their ranks. Semi-solid waste buried most. The escapees fled into piles of elm leaves.

Still squatting, she clutched the wadded newspaper.

"Wondered how long it'd take you to get my scent." Jade eyes unblinking, focused. Faded red lips tight against uneven teeth. "Dollars and cents, big stick."

Krager opened his wallet. "Ready?"

"Depends on what you show me. That's the only arrangement that makes sense."

He handed her two bills, unbuckled his pants. "Dripping yet?"

"I'd give my hundred dollar for an hour's time speech only I'm fresh out of words." She unfurled the blanket. Ants charged toward the hem. She dropped it. "Blanket's infested."

"Do it standing. Do it quick."

She laughed. "Quick is how we like it."

Hands on his shoulders facing him, she lifted into his arms. Flexed thighs embraced him. Heels pounded his butt.

Cradling fingers pinched her ass cheeks. She gasped when he thrust into her, bore down as he slammed against her.

"Know what a whore needs," she said when he let her go.

"Likewise."

"Anything I can wear?"

"In the van."

"Wear your shirt till then?"

"Wear what you have on."

"Which is nothing."

"The old guy hasn't seen a woman. Not since before his wife's funeral. A few years ago."

It started to rain.

Dorn slept through her return. He woke up when she began dressing in the flannel shirt and jeans. The shoes were imitation leather. The shirt was too small, flattening her breasts with the nipples tenting the fabric. The jeans too large; they hid her ripe buttocks.

Pat gave her a clothesline. She used it for a belt.

Dorn blinked sleep crusts. Groaned.

"Boss, you okay?"

"I'm good."

"Kanesville's down the road. Eat there. Shack up back here."

"Share space with bums and wild dogs?" Dorn shook his head.

"It's your money."

Krager U-turned the van, eased over the ruts. On the recently paved highway he tapped the accelerator.

Traffic went the other way. Mostly pickup trucks with muddy skirts.

The sky darkened. The wind picked up.

Dorn turned on the radio.

"Late Autumn flooding has claimed another Iowa town," the news reader said. "Falls Blanche near Des Moines is under twenty feet of runoff from the Iowa River. Anyone who can fill and place a sand bag is asked to report to the Iowa Emergency Management office in the Kanesville Hotel. Pay is ten dollars an hour. You must sign up for ten hours, or more, Now, back to music."

Memphis Minnie sang in a clear, honeysuckle sweet voice: *Me and My Chauffeur Blues.*

When the song ended Kittsy said: "We goin' there?"

"Memphis?" Krager said.

"Kanesville."

"For dinner," Dorn said.

"We could pick up a few bucks, boss, if you weren't in a hurry."

"I'm seventy-five, son. I'm always in a hurry."

"What about me?" she said. "Got no home to flop in."

"Got Mae Hogan's." Pat slowed at the Kanesville city limits.

"She rents by the minute."

"All your family killed back there?" Dorn said.

"Not all. The bastards."

Dorn's eyebrows came down slowly. "Who's left?"

"The old man. Four brothers."

"Uh-huh."

Her voice had a faraway sound. "They hurt me. Real bad."

"When we showed up were they hurting you?" Dorn said.

"No. Brother Bob was working on his car."

"I met his feet," Dorn said.

"Tommy, the electronics genius, was building something."

"What was he building?"

"Something that makes dust out of brick."

"Who else was home?"

"This asshole from Des Moines with the Hitler lip fringe. No relation to me. Wouldn't admit it if he was. No, what he was was a free fuck. Like my family."

Dorn scowled. "Where might they be?"

"No 'might be' about it. On sandbag patrol. That's why they weren't home."

Krager slowed at the traffic light. "We want to find them we need to go down to the river bank."

"Or wait for them to come home," she said. "I won't be there to introduce you."

"Diner over there," Pat said. "Who's hungry?"

"If I was I wouldn't eat there," Dorn said.

"It's what you can afford, Carl."

Dorn grunted.

XI

WHILE THEIR burgers and fries were grilling, Dorn sipped coffee.

Krager rubbed Kittsy's lower back while she read the late edition,

"Stop that." She elbowed his ribs.

He moved to another stool. She showed the headline.

"Meth Lab Explosion Destroys House. Dead Men In Garage Victims of Unknown Assailant."

"We're not unknown," Dorn said.

"Say it louder and make them wonder," Pat said.

The cook turned the burgers. The waitress worked the paper's crossword puzzle.

The trio sat at the counter. No other customers.

"I'm going for a smoke." Krager nodded at the *No Smoking* sign above the counter.

"Gotta do something else." Dorn eased off the stool.

"Something I said?" She didn't smile. Her eyes shone.

The cook called: "Want onions on yours?"

"Lettuce is all." Dorn locked the mens room door.

One stool. No urinal. The sink looked like its original color was black.

He drained, washed, came out.

"Hope nobody was waiting to use it," he told the waitress.

"Yeah, they come for miles to use our restrooms." She served the meal, refilled their cups.

Kittsy tossed the paper on the counter.

Pat Krager came back in and sat at the counter, beyond striking range.

"Any decent hotels around here?" Krager said.

"Two," the waitress said. "Both filled. State emergency officials and sandbaggers. Rent a cot in a lobby'll run ya twenty bucks for the night. If you can find space in the lobby."

"Too cold for camping out unless ya got a sleeping bag and a bottle," the cook said. "Or, a friend."

He eyed Kittsy.

"Careful," Pat said. "She's got a mean elbow."

"Thanks for the warning. Hot apple pie with cheese?"

XII

WHEN THEY LEFT the diner it was four o'clock. The rain stopped. Sentry lights at both ends of the street came on.

A Canadian cold front swept across the north-south street where the van was parked. The few people walking headed toward the town's two hotels. On opposite ends of the four block business district, each seven story brick hotel had a coffee shop and bar.

"Your family drinkers?" Dorn said.

"Weekends only. Not on school nights."

They walked faster. The wind increased. Clouds scudded.

"What're they studying?" Dorn stopped to light a blunt.

"Teaching. Not studying. Dad's a principal of this dinky grade school. Ma taught there, died there during home room. The brothers teach at Council Bluffs Junior High."

Dorn exhaled smoke against her upturned face. Cold stung her eyes, brought tears.

"Know what you're thinking. A family of teachers and one whore. How clunky is that?"

"If it wasn't for sisters like you, and I mean it in the generic sense, I'd still be a virgin," Krager said.

Dorn cupped the blunt. The wind scraped his knuckles.

"After ma died, they made me their whore. Figured, I guess, with her gone, it was open season on her daughter."

Dorn said: "When we showed up?"

She shook her head. "What was on me was that Nazi. The one I told you about. I was in the basement, in the shower, douching, when you showed up. Did you fry that bastard?"

"Did the best we could," Krager said.

They were at the van.

"Hate-pimps teaching our kids," Dorn said. "Scary."

"What's even more so?" Krager unlocked the doors. "Finding a warm shack-up tonight."

When they were in, Dorn said to Kittsy: "Are they survivalists? Would they be in a tent somewhere?"

"They'd be in a hotel with hot water and hotter babes. I don't see their pickups or the van. Not on the street, anyway."

Krager drove to the parking lots adjoining the hotels.

"Nope," she said. "Not here."

He drove north to the few houses clustered off a dirt road, then south to a church, a synagogue and two houses.

"Don't see 'em, fellas."

"They're gone, or sleeping near the river," the old man said.

Krager parked the van under a shedding elm tree behind the diner.

"Where to, boss?"

"Right here. Unless we search by flashlight."

"Can't sleep in the van," Pat said. "Don't mind snuggling. The sheriff might not approve."

"My concern is you, Pat."

"I won't rape her."

"Put money in my hand and rape away." She chewed a hangnail.

"We go back to that abandoned house and you might get torchy," Dorn said. "That's my worry."

"Tell you what you already know, Carl, With me it's a business. Pay me to light a few matches and watch a pro do what he does best. I don't incinerate for the hell of it."

"Makes one of us," she said.

"Pretty good with a torch?" In the mirror above the dashboard the arsonist watched her.

"If I'd had the courage I would've burned them out years ago. That's what I mean."

Their eyes met.

He looked away. "Made those bed springs smoke."

"Stop with the phony baloney imagery, will you?" Dorn said.

"On short notice, boss, it's the best I can do."

"Do something else." Dorn tossed the cigar butt out the window.

Four thirty on the dashboard clock.

"I need a nap," the old man said.

She was about to say something, but didn't.

"After we tuck you in, Carl, don't look for me."

"Where you tuck me in is my concern."

"The hotels?"

"Waste of time."

"People move on."

"Probably a waiting list."

"Speaking of waiting lists," she said. "I've been waiting for you big spenders to make this body an offer." She named her price. "I'll give ya both a ride, and a freebee for breakfast."

"Hey, Carl, how's that for gratitude?"

Dorn frowned.

"Not doing it on the cheap for gratitude. Like you, match man, it's my business."

"Not grateful?" Pat said.

"Sure, I'm grateful. Still my business and since I don't have an 'agent' to do my deals and dream of Heaven. Understand?"

"Let me know if you find Heaven." Dorn massaged his temples.

"Found it. Thanks for that, boys."

"Why didn't you leave?" the elderly man said.

"Tried to." She scratched a chin lesion. "You know who my family is?"

"What they are."

"Exactly who they are. Skinheads. Born over there, in Austria someplace. Dedicated to doing what they do. Get money from another Austrian, this ancient Nazi up in Idaho. The money buys supplies to build the bombs. The old fart in Idaho has a long reach. Last time I left home I got found before I got on the bus. Got dragged back to those animals and got it worse than before I left home. Tell ya something, fellas. If I didn't need the money I'd do ya both till your cocks fell off."

"I'm damn near there," Dorn said. "Sort of."

"Know who that goose stepper is?"

"Emil Nauman," Pat and Carl said.

They exchanged looks. Dorn's was questioning. Krager looked out the side window, blushing.

"Without him we'd all be safer," she said.

"With only the foreign terrorists to fear, how nice the world would be." Krager's laugh was harsh.

"Don't laugh," she said. "This old guy and his kid run this huge organization. He's had close to sixty years to build it. Sixty years since he was brought in, given a lab and staff. He developed these terrible weapons and we used them against the Russkies and everyone else who threatened us. Sixty years, guys. And he's still at it."

"Goose steppers never die," Dorn said. "Without help."

A man in twill with a badge on his coat lapel approached.

Krager keyed the ignition.

XIII

MIDWAY BETWEEN Kanesville and the abandoned farm house, Dorn said, "Pat, how'd you know about Emil Nauman?"

"You told me." He tightened his grip on the wheel.

"Doubt if I did."

A sharp, sideways glance. "What're you saying, Carl?"

"Just asking."

"I read about him in a news magazine. Since my profession doesn't publish monthly journals about the profession, I read news magazines. Or could be I dreamed about him. That's all I can tell you. It'll have to do until I remember exactly."

The smile wrinkled his lips. His eyes were cold.

"Hell, boss, at my age I only half way remember things or forget them entirely."

Krager tapped the brake. The temperature was near freezing. The highway, damp from the rain, was slick.

The elm trees, near the highway, hovered behind barbed wire fences. The moon in a clear sky turned the talonlike branches white.

"Memories," Dorn said.

"What's that, Carl?"

"Nothing."

"Thought you said something."

"The family that slays together, stays together. That's what I said."

"Can't argue with that," Krager said.

"Anybody got a tampon?"

"Aw, shit," Krager said.

Dorn's laugh was a soft, weak sound.

XIV

THEY WAITED in line at Kanesville's pharmacy, behind men and women, silent and unsmiling, in hip boots, bib overalls, flannel shirts, lined jackets and stocking caps. Work gloves protruded from jacket pockets. Their mud-brown clothes smelled of the polluted Iowa River. They bought pint bottles of *Ride 'Em High:* a cheap, two hundred proof regional whiskey. They bought high energy drinks made of sugar and caffeine. They bought copies of the region's largest circulation newspaper to find out how their battle with nature was progressing; their supervisors had no progress reports to give.

"Keep up the good work," the bureaucrats said from a safe distance. "We'll lick it yet."

These skinny, bald men looked more comfortable in white shirts and ties and brown slacks and black shoes.

They wore ankle length wool lined yellow raincoats, hip boots, padded gloves and fake fur hats with ear flaps. Brand new. Bought with tax dollars.

The pharmacy stunk of unwashed bodies, filth-covered clothing, onions and strong coffee and soiled teeth.

Six thirty P.M.

"Gotta do a squat, boss."

"Good luck."

Twenty men formed a line outside the mens room door.

"High point of my day," the retired arson cop said.

"Meet you at the van. If I'm engaged, be kind. Damn, I forgot. She's riding the cotton pony."

"They find a way."

"What goes into her business is her business, boss."

"Was she flowing heavy?"

"How would I know?"

"Your eyes and nose still work?"

"My memory doesn't."

"One box of each, then. If I remember right."

They were in the feminine hygiene aisle.

"Like falling off a bicycle, ain't it, Carl?"

"What is?"

"Buying stuff for a special lady."

"Bought enough."

"Like falling off a bicycle. Once you learn, you never forget."

"I never forgot."

"Okay, boss. See you at the van."

Shopping cart full of tampons and other female products, Dorn started for the checkout counter. Ten people waited. He got in line, dozed standing.

A leg cramp woke him. He walked the aisles to work it out. Traffic was still heavy at the check out.

He found the magazine and newspaper aisle. The region's leading paper was sold out. Next edition at eleven thirty. A few feet away, in a wall rack, was the weekly German language papers *Per Geist Per Stets Verneint.* Translated: "The spirit that never denies." The meaning was buried in Satan worship, and dealt with The Devil's rising.

The paper promoted bund activities in Europe and the United States. The activities were innocent: bake sales to benefit the bund youth sports programs.

That deception hid a deeper meaning. And it sold alongside the Omaha, Nebraska and Des Moines, Iowa daily papers.

He bought the German language weekly. It was published in the United States by the Forslund Nauman Company. He thumbed it. Unable to find a notice announcing the Withersville rally, he folded it, dropped it in the cart.

Something to read if he couldn't sleep.

Two hours between trips for bladder draining.

Once every two hours. Every night.

Midway down the aisle were limited circulation journals. A few copies, photocopied and corner stapled.

He picked up a bound journal. Light green cover. Black lettering of various font sizes.

The lead poem; by contemporary Russian-American Andre Mossovitch was titled:

Package From Hell

> Delivered in the twilight;
> Unopened in an orderly life;
> On a summer porch
> With an open book
> Beside iced tea,
> When love shatters.
> A package from Hell
> Unwrapping in the brain.

He dropped the journal in the cart.

"Something to read," he told the check out clerk.

"Sell a lot of these poetry books. More copies of the German paper than all the newspapers combined. Tells ya something about the region."

"Tells me too much." Dorn used his credit card. Approval was quick.

The others in line up-and-downed this rumpled old man.

"At my age who cares what anyone thinks?" Dorn said to the man behind him.

The man behind Dorn was middle-aged, broad-featured, wisps of gray hair growing from his ears. High forehead partially hidden by a sweat-ringed red and green cap with a dirt-gray bill. Six-six, if he was an inch. Three hundred pounds, most of it muscle.

Bib overalls, flannel shirt, heavy coat that dropped below his knees. Scuffed, muddy boots. He needed a shave.

"Poetry, huh?" said the broad-shouldered man.

"I read anything." The elderly man tried to push past him. The stranger moved into Dorn's path when Dorn moved.

"Seen the newspaper. Thought you was a right-thinking man. Till I seen that poetry crapola." His breath was whiskey thick.

Dorn's eyes watered. His hand moved to the space between the inside of the jacket and the grimy white shirt.

"Okay, Jess?" The store manager appeared beside the checker. "Is he bothering you, sir?"

"No, sir." Dorn kept his hand under his jacket.

"Hell, this old water lily's some kind-ah foreigner." Jess's red rimmed eyes blazed. "A Jew, maybe?"

"Maybe."

"Them cotton ponies fer you?" Jess said.

"Jess, move aside. Let him pass."

To Dorn: "Sorry about this."

"Uh-huh."

Dorn was careful not to step on Jess's toes.

"Damn, Jess," the manager said when Dorn left the line. "The old fart might be a network TV reporter."

"Yeah, I might be an angel," Jess said.

Dorn pushed through the crowd gathered inside the door.

The wind dried Dorn's face, stung his eyes, quieted the rapid heartbeat.

Pickup trucks were parked at the curb in front of the pharmacy, in irregular rows in the side parking lot, under the barren elm in back.

Dorn searched for shadows, found them under the store's overhanging eaves. From there he had a view of the street.

Jess came out, peeling the seal on a pint of *Ride 'Em High.*

A younger man came out behind him, faced him, spoke to him.

Jess shrugged, swallowed whiskey, belched, capped the bottle. The younger man waited for a reply. Jess ignored him. The man followed Jess to the side lot. They passed within six feet of Dorn.

"Now listen, Jess." The younger man reached into a coat pocket. "My wife ain't your property, ain't your business.

And she don't wanna be either one. Now, damn you, show her some respect."

Jess lifted a leg, expelled gas. "That's how much I respect her, you, and all them retards you two gave life to."

"Damn you." The man grabbed Jess's arm.

Jess spun around, facing the man. "Liberal piece-uh crap." He dug a hand in the overall pocket, brought out a switchblade. "Here's how much I respect you and yours."

He advanced, blade held shoulder high. The other man was faster. He ran to within a foot of where Dorn stood. Dorn grabbed the man's arm.

"Let me handle this, son."

Gasping, the man leaned against the shadow covered wall.

Jess advanced, mouth working a soundless litany.

A truck with a damaged muffler sped down the street.

Dorn drew the thirty-eight, aimed, put one steel jacket in the bridge of Jess's flat, veined nose. Pig eyes filled with blood. He staggered back, slid on an ice patch, went down, mouth working.

The truck paused at the intersection before continuing on.

It was quiet, except for the truck's echo.

The man beside Dorn retched, bent over.

"While you're doing that," Dorn said. "Do this."

The old man asked questions. The younger man nodded, answered. "Have a nice night," Dorn said. "Don't look back."

Dorn knocked on the van door. He passed the packages to Kittsy. He sat in the front seat.

"Enjoy your nap?" Dorn said to be saying something.

"She napped. I watched your good work over there. Recognized you in the thirty-eight flash."

"I asked questions. If half the answers are right we're almost ready for Idaho."

"Got a broad in Canada," Pat said. "Right across the border."

"Say, what's all this?" Kittsy said. "Poetry, and . . . And where's the toilet paper?"

"Back in the drug store," Dorn said.

She threw the journal and newspaper in Dorn's lap. "Like to put something else in your lap. Maybe later, huh?"

"Way later," Dorn said.

"Got some booze left, Carl." Krager jockeyed the van over the ice.

"Maybe later."

XV

SEVEN P.M.

Krager put the van in four-wheel drive. The van fought the rutted, muddy road to the abandoned farm house.

No light in the two stories.

"If anyone's home we won't know it until we stumble over the body." Krager got out, slipped, caught himself. "Careful. Slicker than a snot-covered door knob."

"I'm all for staying in the van." Dorn yawned. "Our body heat will keep us from freezing."

Shuddering, she climbed out, stood next to Krager. "Hope you don't hate me. I made a wee mess in there."

The men said: "Uh-huh."

"Could've cleaned me and it if I had toilet paper."

"Do what bums do," Pat said. "Don't worry about it." Then he said: "I have a sleeping bag. For you, Carl. She and me have other plans."

"Like what?" she said.

"Wanna know you better."

"Why?"

"Kids, I talked with a guy back there. He doesn't know your family, Kittsy, but he says he was approached by this really old guy, with bad-fitting false chops."

"Could be him, or who knows how many old men with bad dentures."

"The old putz was beating the drum for the American Nazis. Him and his kin couldn't get rooms in Kanesville. No rooms available. He blamed the government and everyone else for him and the sons sleeping in their vehicles, especially since they came here to help with the sandbagging. He told me where they might be parked. At sunrise we go there, catch them with their pricks in their hands. Then we head north and west."

"Need my third leg massaged," Pat said. "Get you settled, Carl, and then we both sleep."

She held out her hand. He shook it.

"Takes more than that," she said.

Dorn thought a moment. "I was your age, Pat, I walked around half hard all the time. For Milly. Only her. Been a long time."

"Should I be interested?" Kittsy said.

"Take credit cards?"

"Cash and carry."

"No cash."

"No carry."

Krager went to the van, brought out the sleeping bag. It smelled of her discharge. "Stinks a little. Let it air out."

She came over. "We gonna do something or not?" she whispered.

"Not here."

"Okay."

"Don't trip over me," Dorn said. "I'll be by the door."

"Good luck outrunning rats, Carl." Krager picked dust devils, pine needles and elm leaves from the bag.

Dorn took her elbow. "While you clean up your wee mess, describe your family's vehicles."

She let him lead her to the van.

Pat said: "Rags and bleach behind the front seats."

Describing the van and pickups, she scrubbed her wee mess.

The seat of her trousers stretched across her plump, solid buttocks. She moved her hips, looked over her shoulder. Her eyes smoldered.

"Save the visuals for Krager."

"If that's the way you feel."

"Cold in the crotch is how I feel."

While she worked, Dorn joined Pat on the front porch. He pushed the door; it squeaked. Reluctantly, the swollen wood came loose from the surrounding wood molding that formed the doorway.

Dorn brushed cobwebs. Moonlight washed shadows from the entryway and three feet into the front room.

Krager unfolded the bag, spread it across the entrance.

"Come on, boss, I'll wrap you in a blanket, zip you in."

"I can do both, thank you."

"If you need us we will be out and under the moonlight. We won't be gone long."

She tossed the used rags in a weed-choked rose bush.

"Nobody asked me." She came over.

Krager flashed the wallet's contents. "That get your okay?"

"Okay!" She plucked the bills from his hand.

Dorn crawled into the bag.

"Zipper's inside on the right, Carl."

Yawning, the old man nodded.

"Sleep nice, boss."

XVI

DORN AWOKE SUDDENLY, heart racing. His smell choked. He resisted the impulse to cough.

Nine P.M., if his watch was running right.

He unzipped the bag, paused, listened, crawled out.

The air was still. An odor drifted in from the south.

He went to the porch. The van was gone.

Behind him, somewhere in the rear of the house, he heard:

"Only an old man."

"He don't look prosperous," another said.

"Don't look like a bum, either," said a third voice.

A fourth voice: "We keep jabberin' he'll hear us, sure."

Drawing the thirty eight, Dorn carried it outside. He tested the porch's floor boards. Making weak sounds they bent slightly under his weight.

"Hey, where is he?"

"Dunno."

"Mebbe upstairs."

"Fool, we would-ah heard him."

"Especially when he came crashing through them rotted planks up there."

Dorn negotiated space around the overturned porch chair, stopped at the intersecting corner.

The four were inside. No one behind him.

Dorn positioned himself around the corner. He could see the front door and porch without being seen.

Two elm trees, sixty feet high, threw their shadows across the moonlit porch. Darkness touched the porch edge. Dorn remained in shadow.

Footsteps, muffled by dust, made "pah-pah" sounds, and approached the front door.

"There's his bag."

"Where is he?"

"Takin' a piss, most likely."

"Old farts need unloading time."

A shared laugh.

Dorn waited.

They stopped on the porch; they were covered by the trees' shadows. Two men stepped off the porch, into the moonlight.

One directed his urine stream at the other man's shoe tops.

He jumped back, almost falling. "Hey, dick hole."

"Just watch me work," said the pisser.

The rapid gruff noise coming from him sounded like laughter.

"When you're alone you put it where you can," wet shoes said. "But, damn you, I just got these at that hobo hotel in Omaha."

The men on the porch moved, directionless, in and out of the light.

They were tall, scrawny, almost lost in clothes too large for their small-boned frames.

No weapons visible.

They looked around, looked at each other. Then stepped off the porch. One pointed to tire tracks in the mud.

"Bulls from town?"

"One cop in Kanesville."

"Seen civilians in vans in town. Sheriff rides a city issued car. Big assed insignia on both doors."

"Lookin' like a pizza delivery truck."

Shared laugh.

"Ain't worried about who *was* here. Only what's out here now."

"Where the hell is he?"

"Must be takin' one ass-sore crap."

"Scoop his litter in a bag, use it for sandbaggin' the levee down there."

Shared yawn.

"Talkin' 'bout levees puts me in mind of grunt labor, fill-in', haulin' sandbags."

"Makes me weary just thinkin'."

"Fillin', haulin' in this weather. Done my share when I had to do it. Sure didn't care much. Freezin' weather's bad as doin' it when it's ninety degrees, and the only shade is when ya blink."

"When did you do stoop labor?"

"When we was all doin' a dime in Joliet."

"Seems like I remember."

"Hell fire, young-un, you can't remember your last drink."

"Way too long ago."

"Bottle's in my bindle."

"Find this ancient scratcher first. Drink later."

"Got an itchy throat right now."

"We spread out, or what?"

"Better spread out."

"For all we know he done died passing the turd from Hell."

"Yeah, he should be back here by now."

"Dammit, we should-uh jumped him when we seen him. An hour ago and we could be havin' that drink right now."

"We was havin' that drink an hour ago which is why we didn't. Case you forgot."

"All this jive-ass scared him to the highway."

"Wonder where his car is?"

"No footprints I can see."

"Maybe he came down from up there."

"Tree tops or Heaven?"

"Old men don't climb trees and sinners never get to Heaven."

"I'm losin' beauty sleep jivin' about him."

"Been ugly too long for beauty sleep to help."

"Last night you said I was purdy."

"Find him. Ask him how he got here."

"One foot in front of the other, most likely."

"Most likely," they said.

The porch floor squeaked.

The four, grouped around the tire tracks, looked around.

Dorn stepped out, firing.

The two closest to the porch crumpled, faces forward.

The second pair, standing in the muddy tracks, tensed, looked to their fallen comrades, to the porch. They crouched ready to flee.

Dorn moved to the porch edge, firing, counting discharges.

The two did an uncoordinated, backward ballet, legs lifting, jerking, Arms waving. Mouths slightly moving.

On their backs, they thrashed, whimpered.

Dorn re-loaded, kicked ribs, got no response until he reached the one sprawled, hands grubbling air, lungs laboring.

"Any more in there? Tell me. You'll live."

Blood from his nose and ears flecked his black-white shaggy beard.

"Aw Lord, man. Help me first." His fingers clenched, relaxed.

"Playing the street-smart chump right to the bullet to the brain. Fool." Dorn put a steel jacket in the bum's left eye.

His head slammed back. Mud squished. Fingers became fists that quickly relaxed.

Dorn went inside.

Moonlight came through the gaps in the roof, made white squares on the floor, highlighted dust that drifted from his footfalls.

Sleeping bags were spread on the kitchen floor, in the rear. Back packs were piled in a corner. Ignoring the stink he shook the contents on the floor.

Cigarettes, bottles with a few drops in each, toilet paper. Straight razors, pen knives, switch blades, pepper spray, a paperback original: *The Arson Job,* copyrighted 1978, written by Jack Moss, an author whose promise was never realized.

"What does a jerk-off writer know about arson?"

Finally, what he searched for.

A mimeographed one-sheet:

"Tired of being duped, scammed by the government? Ready for a change? Withersville, Idaho is where you need to be on November 24, 2008. We will meet outside the Withersville Bus Depot on South Street, east of the town square. Let's form a phalanx of solidarity, bumper to bumper, from the bus depot to the meeting hall. You provide your transportation. We will provide the incentive. Together we can clean up Washington. We will show you how."

"Thanks for the way in," Dorn told the night.

He pocketed the one sheet.

He went out on the porch. The stink blowing from the south had dissipated. The wind died. The chill made breathing difficult. The air, tasting like pepper, made him cough.

"Which explosive smells like pepper?"

Krager would know.

XVII

THE VAN'S HEADLIGHTS swung around the curve, onto the road, bouncing with each rut. The van stopped inches from the first body.

When Krager got out, he looked around. "What the . . ."

"Guess who came to dinner?" The blanket covered Dorn's shoulders. "Guess who ate the guests?"

Kittsy stopped outside the cone of moonlight illuminating the dead. "They don't look gnawed on." A nervous, childlike laugh.

Krager went to the porch where Dorn waited.

"They commit suicide?"

"Might say they did."

"Damn, Carl, you really know how to dish it out. A spoon at a time."

Krager's clothes smelled like pepper.

Dorn sneezed.

"Bless you," she said.

"He closed His eyes long time ago." Dorn brought out the sheet. "Give this your editorial eye, Pat."

Krager unfolded it. "What's this?"

"What I hoped for."

"The secret of a long life? What?"

Shivering, she got back in the van.

Dorn said: "My money man thought the goose-steppers might hold their convention in Withersville. Now we know."

"I could pass for one," Pat said. "But, you . . ."

"We surprise them. They won't notice me."

"That beard you're raising makes you look like an oldtime rabbi."

"Like my grandfather, father. Dachau put an end to the calling." Krager pursed his lips, exhaled, said nothing. The sunglasses reflected the moon's glow.

"Smell like pepper," the old man said.

"Smell like onions, too. We stopped for burgers."

The wind came from the north, from Canada. Odors and fumes were swept south. Occasional smoke wisps dodged the rushing chill, hovered above Kanesville's south side.

A siren's faint keening rose, abruptly dropped.

"Something going on south of here," Dorn said. "Doing what you do, Patrick?"

"Screwing her is what I did. Bought food after." He fired up a blunt. The tip glowed. Smoke hung between them.

Dorn's back was damp. He folded the blanket, held it against his chest like a lifeline.

"We've always been honest with each other," he said.

"Want a recap of all the stuff we did?"

"What you did. So I know where your head is."

"Where it's always been. On business."

"Free lancing on my dollar?"

"I did a job. Hired weeks ago. Before Manvitz. Before this pilgrimage. That's what you need to know, boss."

"On this pilgrimage as you call it trust has to be there."

"I trust you to pay my fee. You trust me to do what needs to be done. And, yeah, I did a job an hour ago. For a developer who wants land on the cheap. Vacant lots sell cheaper than lots with houses on them. The client's name is private." He examined his watch. "After ten. Past my bed time. Need me to tuck you in?"

"I can handle a sleeping bag."

"Just being friendly."

Dorn grunted.

Krager climbed into the van. In the moon's light Dorn applied lubricant to the catheter. When he came out of the bushes Kittsy waited on the porch. The iron chair was upright. She stood beside it, gestured.

"Have a seat, Mr. Dorn. Need to talk to you about something."

XVIII

LEVEN P.M.

She waited for his answer.

Dorn thought it over before he said: "I'm too old to be any one's bodyguard. After I find your family I put the gun away. Pat can handle a weapon good as me, better than me."

"I didn't make myself clear. I don't want a bodyguard."

"What do you want?"

"Jews are good businessmen. I need a Jew to take care of my business. The messy side of business. A man who appreciates a dollar, and the opportunity to make a dollar, honestly or otherwise. Has the balls and know—how to make it happen. And, if need be, protect my interests." She looked around. A curtain of mosquitoes hung between the porch and the bodies. "Four in a row while me and the fire bug were doing it. Impressive, Mr. Dorn. The fire fly wasn't so bad, either."

"I'd take my bow sitting down only my bladder hurts and I'm too tired to do it, standing."

She leaned over. He inhaled onions, rotting teeth, armpits and crotch. He hadn't smelled a woman's crotch since before Mildred died.

"Just making conversation, Mr. Dorn. I know arson cops are paper shufflers. Where did you learn to shoot?"

"In 1946 I was taken in by an Austrian family. He was a cop."

"Doesn't answer my question."

"No, it doesn't." Standing, he massaged his tail bone. "Unlike a hard life we can always exit a hard chair. Without worrying about Heaven."

"Sleeping inside?"

"I won't sleep."

"Room for two in that bag."

"I have an uncertain bladder."

"What you need . . ."

"Is a new prostate."

"I got the end-the-blues guarantee right down here." She touched herself.

"I got cancer."

"It isn't contagious."

"Just painful."

"All kinds of pain in this life. People like us, Mr. Dorn. We play the wrong cards, pick the wrong numbers."

"Probably right." Hand on the door, he hesitated.

Her brows lifted. A small smile crossed thin, pale lips.

"Something you wanna say, Mr. Dorn?"

"Yeah, Stop calling me Mr. Dorn. Name's Carl. Not Mr. Carl. Just plain Carl."

"Okay, just plain Carl."

"I can enjoy a little joke. Very little enjoyment."

"Suits your friend."

"In the next life, maybe," Dorn said. "Pat torched something tonight."

"Two one-story shacks. South end. The shacks book-ended a church and synagogue. Strange. A church and synagogue side by side."

Dorn lit a blunt. His hand shook. "Yeah. Strange."

XIX

DORN SPENT THE NIGHT, inside, sitting on the sleeping bag, the blanket around his shoulders. He smoked, coughed, drained his bladder, frowned.

He said to himself: "My first kill. I was thirteen. Considered a man by my people. Stepdad, after a beating, after I begged him to stop, admitted he marched for Herr Hitler, that Hitler should have succeeded. Got his side arm. Shot him while he slept. His wife had her own bedroom and sleeping pills. I opened the window across the room from his bed. I dropped the two shell casings outside, on the balcony. Police looking for an easy solution blamed the murder on an enemy who climbed a ladder. His wife mourned long and loud until the first pension check arrived. She bought new clothes and a spa membership. Started seeing younger men. Men that didn't want a kid underfoot. She put me in an orphanage. Helluva way to start puberty. I faked normal behavior. Kept his gun nearby, hidden, oiled and loaded. Hatred never dies. Mine. Theirs. Hitler lovers lived unless they were within range of that weapon."

His bladder cramped.

Four A.M.

In the bushes, Krager did what Dorn needed to do.

"A good lay," Pat said. "A better piss. What better way to spend an early morning. Right , Carl?"

"Let me do what I need to do."

"Modest in your old age?"

"Might say so, and you just did."

"When do we leave?"

"Now."

Dorn tossed the sleeping bag in the van. Kittsy stirred, wiped her nose, belched, slept.

Krager keyed the ignition.

"Huh?" she yawned. "Time?"

"Four," Dorn said.

"Too damn early."

"Not if you're homeless and helpless." Krager made a U-turn, left the lights off until they reached the highway. "Where to, boss?"

"Coffee."

"Convenience store this side of the bridge."

"I'm hungry," she whined.

They dodged her morning breath.

"Got to wash," she said. "Smell like I took on a regiment on one douche."

"Convenience store has one crapper," Krager said.

"Most of them only have one," she said.

"Might find a man in there doing what men do when they're alone," Pat said.

"An opportunity for me."

They ate donuts and coffee in the van.

She snapped her fingers.

"Already paid you," Krager said.

"This is down payment on the future."

Krager tossed a five dollar bill over his shoulder.

She got out. "Back before ya know I'm gone."

"We'll know."

They fanned air. Krager with his hand; Dorn with the German language newspaper.

Kittsy came out with a travel bag. She crossed in front of the van to the bathroom a few feet away. An elm copse was a few feet beyond that.

Krager watched her walk. "She sure knows how to sell the merchandise."

"Economy's bad. Her market's always good."

After she went in, a pickup drove up, parked near the bathroom. A man, hump-backed, walking slowly, tried the bathroom door.

"About done in there?" He pounded the door.

"Levee worker," Pat said. "Or he enjoys mud wallowing."

"Don't remember your being so talkative."

"Prime pussy lubricates the tongue."

"I guess she is young."

"Between the legs."

"They learn fast."

"Miss it?"

"Miss my wife."

"Seemed nice. Your Molly."

"Mildred."

"Milly. Never treated me like I was a jailbird."

"She never treated me like I was an underpaid civil servant in a dead-end job."

"Make your opportunities. I did."

"We lived in one room apartments. In the basement. She kept the place clean, kept out the ants, cockroaches, garter snakes. Couldn't keep out the cold. More cracks in the walls than wine drinkers in France. That was our life. Couldn't afford a burial plot. Donated her body to the medical school. Should've tied in with the Nazi hunters before now. Might've made her life a bit more pleasant." He looked across the seat. "Her death less humiliating. But, who knows?"

"Talk about talkative." Pat removed the sun glasses, rubbed the red rims framing the yellow irises. The whites were black and red veined.

Pat consulted his watch. Five fifteen.

"She must've fallen in."

"Was she carrying a newspaper?"

"Don't recall." The hunchback paced in front of the bathroom door.

Silently swearing, he slammed a fist against the steel barrier.

"Get off the pot!"

The door swung wide.

"Bastard!" She sprayed toothpaste.

Her blouse was open. She didn't wear or need a bra.

The old man stared.

"Well, look-eeee here." He drooled. "I've seen these beauties before."

"Hello, pa. Toothless fuck."

"Don't I? Hee-hee-hee." He reached.

She stepped back in the doorway.

Krager opened the van door.

Dorn passed him the thirty eight.

"Gimme some sugar, sugar." Fingers grubbled air above her breasts.

Her eyes glinted. "Sure, pappy."

He giggled, gasped, eyes widening. Tongue darted over sagging lips A stain, spreading across his crotch, mingled with mud spots.

"Kittsy." His voice skittered.

She took his arm, turned him toward the trees. Over her shoulder, she shook her head. Krager stopped. The thirty eight was at his side.

In the copse, she dropped her pants.

"Want it, daddy? All wet and warm for ya." Her voice caressed.

"Yessss . . ." He struggled with the bib overalls. "Sugar, you were always my best bounce."

He jerked the overalls over his sagging belly.

"Even better than your ma." His pants gathered around his boot tops. "Got talent, you have," he growled.

She clenched her fist. The nail file from the travel kit abraded her palm. He moved toward her, nearly tripping over the bunched bibs.

He stumbled, shrieked: "Bitch! Help me!"

"Will do, old man." She gripped the file's flat end.

Her arm shot forward. The tip and most of the shaft disappeared in his right eye socket. No blood yet. No reaction. The left eye showed surprise and that was it.

She kicked his right knee. He fell back. She knew which pocket contained the bone-handled switchblade. He thrashed like a fish on a boat dock, yelping, cursing, sobbing, babbling. His cock lay on his thigh like a dead eel washed up on a dirt-gray dune. Yellow-white ooze dribbled over his thigh and knee.

The blade clicked.

He yowled, helpless.

"This is for the good times." She unmanned him.

His screams were short, rapid gasps. He trembled, voided.

Before the blood and waste from the eye socket reached the shirt pocket, where his wallet was, she found the faded brown fake leather wallet, took fifty dollars in small bills—all there was—and the truck keys.

"Say hello to Satan, bitch." She pocketed the money.

Leaves snapping behind her turned her around.

Krager tucked the thirty eight behind his belt.

"I was gonna come in, shooting and rescuing. It looks like the old one's in need of rescuing, but I think he's beyond rescuing now."

He shuddered, whimpered. Flesh around his mouth darkened.

"A breath or three left in his evil self. Screw it. Let him bleed it out." She pointed. "Fire ants got his stink."

"Let's not disturb them."

Her pants were still around her knees.

"Airing out your talent?"

"Waiting for the five A.M. rush." She pulled them up.

"Past five." He dropped an arm around her shoulder.

She snuggled, her hand on his manhood.

When they came out of the elm copse they looked like lovers on a pre-dawn walk.

Except for the van and pickup the lot was empty.

"Don't think our old man heard anything, or gave a damn if he did." Pat opened the driver's side door.

Dorn woke, looked around. "What about the car?"

"Boss, you're sitting in it."

"His car. Or truck. Whatever he drove here."

"Parked over there."

"The rest of them are close by," she said. "Sleeping, most likely."

Dorn said: "Where's herr old guy?"

"Ant feast." She brought him up to date.

Krager turned the ignition key. "Wanted to save him for you, Carl. Only she was having too much fun."

"Five left," she said. "I drive the pickup."

Dorn said: "Got your license, Kittsy?"

"When you pulled me out of there was I carrying one?"

"I take the pickup." Dorn got out.

Pat said: "He came up on the south road."

A mile down the flat, two-lane macadam road Dorn pulled onto a hard dirt secondary. Krager parked behind the pickup.

They got out.

A van and pickup, one behind the other, rested on a rock shelf across the road, over a drainage ditch.

"There they are," she said.

A pulse beat in her throat and temple.

Her eyes glinted.

XX

A CLOUDLESS PRE-DAWN. The moon receded. The macadam road was empty of traffic. The trio stood in the middle lane.

Krager said: "Time to suit up."

Pat returned to the van, came back with the rocket launcher on his shoulder and missiles in a box in his hand.

"Not yet," Dorn said. "They might be off taking a sit-down."

"Wouldn't they follow the old man to the store?"

"They might," she said. "Coffee and a crap's their morning routine. Don't much care where they are when it's crap time."

Overhanging tree limbs threw enough shadow to hide in.

On cue, Krager and Kittsy took to the trees.

Dorn was alone in the road's middle, a fixed smile an ugly upturn of his lips.

The truck's driverside door opened. The overhead light went on. The driver unzipped his fly, directed the piss into the road's midsection. Dorn, darting out of the way, caught the pisser's attention.

When Dorn moved he bumped into Kittsy.

She was at his side. "That's the mean one. Vic's his name."

Dorn moved slightly. Her toothpaste hadn't done its job.

Movement inside the truck.

"Probably Wendell in there. He and Vic have this unholy arrangement."

Vic snarled: "What da fuck do ya want?"

Thirty-eight in hand, with his hand in his coat pocket, Dorn approached. Kittsy walked behind the elderly man.

"Where the hell did you come from?" Vic's face was bloated. His eyes were shielded by his squint. "What do ya want?"

The shotgun was between his legs. The muzzle, touching the steering column, was two inches above the window's sill.

Dorn stopped. "My bus ran out of go-juice back there at the convenience store."

"Panhandling at this hour?" Vic's laugh woke the robins in their nests and Vic's passenger from his dream.

Wendell said: "Dammit, Vic. I was havin' this sweet dream."

Vic said: "Got ourselves a lost soul in need. Wants us to help him get home."

"To the levee is all." Dorn stepped back. "Sorry if I disturbed your sleep."

Vic whispered to his brother. They laughed. The doors opened. Yawning, Wendell hesitated at the passenger's open door. Vic was at the other door. The shotgun was pointed at Dorn.

"Ever been gang-shagged by real men with rape ideas?"

"Only real thing you losers have is your stomachs," came from behind Dorn.

Kittsy stepped out of Dorn's shadow.

"What . . ."

"Duh . . ."

She took Dorn's arm. "Where's Ortha and Tommy and Jess?"

"Asleep." Wendell's voice cracked.

"Where?"

"In the van." Shotgun hip high, Vic approached. "Leastways Jess is in there."

Twenty feet separated them.

"Ortha and Tommy are down there," Vic said. "With the other sandbaggers." He gave her the up and down. "Sure look fine, Kit." His pants bulged. "Them other two don't know what they're missin'."

"Ain't got it yet." She slammed against Dorn, throwing him to the ground. "Any time, Pat," she yelled, on top of Dorn.

Krager put a load into the truck's front end where the brothers stood. The concussion shook the ground. Dorn and Kittsy rode the shock waves until they became screams of steel and robins, then settled in a rainstorm of debris.

Dorn and the girl covered their heads.

The sounds settled. The storm subsided. Flames lashed the trees, branches became embers piling around the truck and van, and the charred bodies in the road.

From the open van door, Jess fired, striking trees across the road.

"Must not be wearing his glasses," she said.

"Jess, honey. Don't shoot. It's Kittsy. Let me see you."

"Kittsy?" His voice trebled.

He got out, head swinging right, left.

"Oh, there you are." He lowered the rifle.

"He's mine." Dorn rolled on his side, facing Jess. Four steel jackets perforated his navel, diaphragm, left lung and throat.

Jess did an uncoordinated dance in place before falling back. His head struck the van's front bumper.

"Three gone to glory." Krager helped them off the road and into his van.

Who's keeping score?" she said.

"All of us," Dorn said.

"How many left, boss?"

"Two."

XXI

THE WORK LIGHTS buzzed. They drew the last of the summer moths.

The levee stretched seven miles north, nine miles south.

Portable generators powered the work lights. The lights were mounted on poles driven into the ground and held there by concrete bases.

Farther back, near the road leading to the work area, were equipment storage trailers, a portable kitchen, and tents for rest periods.

The constant grind of men talking, trucks and earth movers working, made them shout.

"See them?" Dorn said.

"Close as we are I'd have to be blind not to," she said. "If they were here."

They stood on the road. Thirty feet below were two dozen laborers filling, tying, stacking sandbags on flatbed trucks.

Bags on both banks of the Iowa River reinforced the levee.

A flatbed carrying men from town bounced over the ruts. The horn's blast cleared the road: a two-lane dirt road dead-ending at river's edge.

The truck stopped there. The workers jumped off, were given cards to sign, had their IDs checked, were issued shovels and taken to the pile. Empty bags waited there.

"Got to lose a load, guys," she said.

"You smell interesting," Pat said.

"So nasty," she said, over her shoulder.

"We all need to be something."

When she went into the copse on the far side of the north-south road, Pat said: "Carl, when do we go after this?"

"After this."

"What do we use?"

"What do you mean?"

"No cannons. Unless you want my launcher."

"She finds them, I do the rest. Up close."

"Carl, in my business the greater the distance, the better."

"In yours, maybe."

The wind picked up, penetrated Dorn's coat.

Krager zipped the fleece-lined jacket.

At first light the work lights went off.

"Any pictures?" Krager said.

"One of Mildred. Wallet sized."

"No pics of the Vreelanders?"

"Photos when they were kids and the old man had hair and a straight back. Nothing recent. Descriptions are all."

"So we could've roamed the countryside looking for people we couldn't ID."

"I planned on doing the family at their crib. This side trip's costing me energy. Hope it's well spent."

"Her being here might save us time."

Dorn's bladder throbbed. "Hopefully."

"Her and me. It won't get complicated."

Dorn coughed mucus. "A whore isn't much to come home to."

"Who said I'd come home to her?" Krager said.

Dorn tightened his sphincter, trapping the urine.

"Try getting rid of her."

Dorn started for the copse.

Krager walked with him. "Like watching the same porn film. After awhile you need other porn films. She goes back to Mae Hogan's and the world keeps turning."

They crossed the road.

"She's got plans. Including you or not, Pat. She never said. She also never said what she wanted me for. Not specifically. Take away my one ability and I'm another old man, weeping on street corners, begging for coffee and cake. Be like that before she has her grand plan paid for. It must be something I'm needed for right row. Don't know what it is."

"Didn't know she had plans."

"Don't sign over your life insurance."

They stopped in front of the trees.

"That Kanesville job," Dorn said.

"Hell, Carl. They're just buildings."

"It's what they signify."

"Already told you why the job got my personal touch."

"A church and synagogue."

"Nobody attends either one. They drive into Council Bluffs or Omaha."

Dorn winced. "Got to drain my circus tent."

"Something I said?"

"Something I drank."

Kittsy came out of the copse.

"Save a dry spot for me?" Dorn said.

"Be careful where you put your size elevens."

His bladder cramped.

He entered the copse.

Sweat felt like ice drops on his forehead. Tree branches, grouped like the bones of Dachau's living dead, closed in.

He sagged against an elm, pulled himself up, oiled the rubber tube.

A bolt of pain when the catheter struck the prostate.

The gland was swollen. It refused to yield. Slight pressure and the catheter passed the gland. Suddenly reddish black liquid rushed, jerking the tube, splattered the leaf fist flexed against the trunk. Drops dotted tips of his worn, discount house shoes. The light brown fake leather turned black.

Liquid waste soaked the leaves. Run off backed up, drained over the shoe tips. Sour odors made his nose twitch, made his last meal rise. The stink was like a public urinal's fumes.

Abruptly, the flow stopped.

He retracted the rubber pony. A spoon's worth squirted against the trunk. The catheter, when it came out, dripped blood.

He slipped it into its paper sheath.

"Screw the germs."

Infections were the least of his worries.

"Everything come out okay?" Krager said.

"Okay." Dorn said to Kittsy: "Seen anyone?"

"Not yet. Eating or sleeping. What they do best." She pointed to a row of vehicles parked parallel to the dirt road. "Their pickup's over there. Nothing going on that I can see from here."

"Checked it out, close up?"

"Naw. The guys down there might put me to work. They can't afford, from their looks, what I do best."

Dorn came up alongside Krager.

"Boss, I think you . . ."

"Accidents happen."

"You guys think your stinks are my favorite odors."

"Put her on the payroll, Carl. Might make things sweeter."

"Folks," the old man said, "stop with the foreplay, or afterplay, whatever you're doing."

"Jive ass, boss, is the universal language."

She squinted. "Look pale, Carl."

"Need Vitamin D."

Wind from the north came up, rippled the river. The sky darkened.

"Do it like we talked about." Dorn checked the thirty-eight's chamber.

Krager went to the van. Kittsy went down the road to the cook tent, looked in, shook her head. The break tent was next to the portable kitchen.

Nothing.

The latrine, a tent with portable sinks with mirrors attached, and portable toilets and a urinal, was between the main access road and the elm trees.

She climbed the road, stopped in front of Dorn.

"They aren't eating or sleeping so they have to be shitting."

She led the way to the men's latrine.

Ortha and Tommy were on the pot. Ortha, heavier than his brother, read the German language paper. Tommy, skinny, undernourished, dozed. His bony legs were spread-eagled.

Diabetic sores dotted the calves. Ortha's legs were hairless, white, flabby.

When Kittsy entered, Ortha looked up. "What the crap?"

"Don't get up, bro."

"Wasn't planning to."

One of the newly arrived laborers came in, lit a cigarette, hummed as his bladder emptied. He ignored the others.

"Took him longer to unzip his fly than it did to drain it," Dorn said to himself.

Kittsy said when the intruder left: "Guys, I want you to meet a friend."

Tommy mumbled. His eyes stayed shut.

Ortha gave the elderly man the up and down, grimacing.

"Your friend a foreigner, sis? Or, worse?"

"Worse," Dorn said. The thirty-eight filled his hand. "This is the day you meet Hitler."

Ortha stood, pants around his ankles, face reddish white. He reached for his pants, cursing in German. He reached for the ankle holster, groped, looked down for it. Dorn put two steel jackets into the top of his naked skull.

Tommy woke, dazed, drooling.

Kittsy embraced him. "It's all right, dear. Everything's aw-right."

"That you, Kit? That noise? Who's he?"

"Your sister's problem solver," Dorn said.

Kittsy was at the entrance.

The old man said: "Open wide, kid." He shoved the muzzle into the young Nazi's mouth.

The blast threw him back. Then he pitched forward. His eyes showed surprise. His nose, cheeks and jaw were gone.

Humming, Dorn wiped the muzzle on a coarse brown paper towel.

Moistening a towel, he daubed parts of Tommy from his coat and forehead. As an afterthought, he washed the catheter.

She had already fled.

The temperature dropped from a tolerable forty-eight degrees to a breath-stopping twenty-eight. The wind sighed steadily. She was up on the road by Krager and the van.

"What about their trucks?" she said. "Paid for."

"Got gas money?"

"Not that much."

"There's your answer."

Voices from the latrine. Men rushed past them.

"If we had time," Pat said. "We could siphon."

"The old war criminal's gas gauge was on empty," Dorn said. "We're stuck. Together."

"Lord," she said, "I won't ride with you stinking like you do, Carl."

"Walking's good exercise," he said. "We're going through Omaha. Drop you wherever you want."

"Or you can stay with us," Pat said.

"Okay," she said.

"That okay, Carl?"

"Fine."

An unbroken cloud overhead thickened.

Krager turned on the radio.

"A pre-Thanksgiving Day blizzard is fast approaching," the news reader said. "Good news for property owners along the Iowa River. A rapid freeze is expected. Some crews have been dismissed. Stay tuned to this station for weather updates."

"We best find shelter," Dorn said. "Kanesville's probably booked. Council Bluffs has the casinos and the outrageous prices, and I'm close to my credit limit. So it's Omaha."

"The asshole of the world," she said. "Well, it's good for something."

"Which is?" Krager said.

"High taxes."

"Like calling Hitler a humanitarian," Pat said.

Dorn winced. "I need a doctor. Fast."

XXII

A T EIGHT A.M. Krager dropped Dorn at Omaha's St. Swivvens Hospital emergency entrance.

"We'll find us a hotel. Come back and pick you up right here." Krager put the van in reverse.

The elderly arson cop shivered. His temperature equaled his age. Temperature outside dropped another ten degrees. The wind was a steady twenty miles an hour from the north.

He registered at the front desk, showed his state employees insurance card, filled out a form, and waited.

Nine A.M. a nurse escorted him to an exam room, asked questions, took his temperature and blood pressure, and left.

He sat on the exam table, then curled up on it and was almost asleep when a male nurse came in.

He handed Dorn a porcelain urinal. "If you need to pee."

"Any idea when the doctor might show up?"

"Short staffed. She's got an emergency down the hall. Two homeless men duked it out. Another one got knifed over a bottle and a babe. Two husbands, one wife and a loaded twenty-two. You're number six."

Dorn and the urinal were alone.

The intern, a husky young blonde with short hair came in, glanced at his paperwork, oiled her gloved finger.

"Pull 'em down, hon. Turn on your side."

He bit his lip.

Her finger went in, palpated the gland, withdrew. She tossed the latex glove in a waste receptacle.

"Don't need to tell you what the problem is. I recommend surgery. Soon. Before it spreads to the spine, kidneys."

"I'm bypassing surgery, going directly to hospice care."

"Your decision."

"Write me a prescription?"

"Won't help."

"Now is not a good time for cutting."

"Never is. Listen to me. You can live without your go-gland. You'll need to learn certain procedures, like how to retain urine so you don't embarrass yourself and offend others. Learning to control bladder function is easy. A cancer death is not. But it's whatever you want."

"I want to be fifty again."

"I'd like to have a cock. Won't happen, either."

"Guess it won't."

She signed the paperwork. "Drop these at the reception desk. I'd do it but they need me down the hall in the opposite direction. Another oldster who refuses surgery." She gave him a hard look, "Right now you're not terminal. I don't think. Without x-rays it's difficult to know how advanced the cancer is. Your guy-gland feels almost tumor-free. That's why I recommend surgery now. Before it becomes a needless expense. No sense paying for a urologist's country club membership. Well, sir, best of luck."

He followed her out, took the opposite turn in the hall, to reception, and then outside.

Thirty mile an hour wind from the north nearly knocked him over. So strong it choked breath, pierced the coat and undergarments, needling wet flesh.

"Pat, where the hell are you?" he said.

XXIII

KRAGER AND KITTSY registered as a married couple at the downtown Windsor Hotel: four floors of clean rooms with clean linen and free soap and faded flower designs on the walls.

"Been in worse." She dropped her jacket on one of two arm chairs.

"Found you in worse," Krager said from the bathroom. "Wonder how Carl's doing?"

"I don't keep track of people. Jews especially."

He came out, wiping his hands. "Washed my digits. Didn't hear you."

"Didn't say anything worth hearing. Got time for a quickie?"

"You're still riding . . ."

"Riding the cotton pony. Yeah, I'm in my period. I'm not dead."

"Well . . ."

"Can't do the missionary. How about the harmonica?"

"Play it like Jazz Gillum?"

"Name the tune."

"Anything in the key of F."

She pulled down his pants. "Whew!"

"I didn't wash. So?"

She shrugged. "Smelled worse."

She squatted on the air mattress, pumped his penis.

"Like riding a surf board, sitting down," she said. "Whee!"

Grunting, he tried to engage her, freed himself, dropped on the bed beside her, fell asleep.

"Sure know how to make a lady feel wanted." She climbed off.

In the bathroom she finished herself off, put on her trousers. Sat in the arm chair under the pole lamp.

She was halfway through the throw-away publication; *Guide to Omaha's Affordable Attractions* when he woke up.

"What's that?" He licked dry lips.

"A hundred blank pages. We can watch the homeless booze it up in the bus shelters. No charge for that."

He sat up, rubbed his face. "Sorry. Showing my age."

"Shmuck mid shlag." Her face was expressionless.

"Sounds nasty."

"Not nasty. Disappointing."

"Speak German?"

"Why?"

"What you just said. With the accent you sound like you speak it."

"Heard it enough at the house."

"Sauerkraut's the only German I know. Helps when I order bratwurst."

"I could use some of that. Double portion."

"Need to get Carl."

"Have a few dollars you're not using? For food?"

"We're eating on his dime."

"He controls the money?"

"His party."

"Figures. They own all the money. Don't they?"

"Who does?"

"Never mind."

"I do mind."

"Don't. Not important."

"Got some of your dad in you."

"Had some, yeah. Straight in. To my tonsils which he violated from the other end."

"Carl isn't cheap."

"A slur is based on fact. Always." She glared.

"He doesn't blame all the Germans for Hitler."

"Yeah? Well, maybe he should. Want my back door?"

He zipped his pants. "Got to go."

She looked out the window. "Blizzard's coming."

"Stay here."

"Snowed in by myself? Nope." She went for her jacket.

On the elevator, she said: "I'm bloated. Crampy. Got a headache. Hungry. Worried about the next job. When I'm like that—all moonstormy—I'm not nice. I don't hate Carl. Offered him a job. He tell you?"

"Not much."

"Not much to tell yet. You, me and him might make pretty decent money together."

They crossed the lobby to the parking lot entrance.

In the van he turned on the heater. The motor warmed.

"Not interested in running a cat house," he said.

"I'm hanging up my fuck shoes and thongs. Going into another scheme. A political one."

"Running for city dog catcher?"

"Not that kind of politics."

"Cross burning in corn fields?"

"Hell, son, that went out with southern moonshiners and northern revenuers."

"I was hoping."

"What were you hoping, Pat?"

"Cross burning throws a little light. Not much. Little is better than wall to wall darkness."

"You like burning things on cold cloudy nights."

"Kind-ah cozy, ain't it?"

She nodded, a small smile dimpling her cheeks.

"I could've been real useful over there in one of those camps, stoking furnaces."

"It was fun, if you were dedicated."

"Male prisoners worked the mines."

"High born broads with fat asses and sagging tits danced naked for the high command and when that got boring the officers tossed them to the enlisted men. Then, later, the furnaces."

"Sure wish I could've done some stoking at Dachau or some other camp."

"You'd be toast now. Unless you ducked. Not getting caught's the secret. Daddy and the brothers never learned that. Went out, recruiting. The cause goes on. With men and women focused, cautious, smart. Who know how to work the system. Make the system work for the cause."

Eleven thirty.

The lunch crowd waited on corners for the traffic lights.

She turned. "Hot roast beef with gravy and mashed potatoes crank your crank?"

Eyes on the swirling snow spiraling across the windshield, he nodded.

XXIV

DORN STEPPED OUT from under the doorway's protective stone cover.

Krager listened to the all news station.

"Bitter cold from Canada will stick around for the next two days," the news reader said. "An inch of the white stuff will make your drive time commute a bit slick. Good news: no additional snow expected. That could change. Stay tuned."

"Get us comfortable rooms?" Dorn said.

"Bed didn't look ticky. Did it, Kits?"

"Didn't see any. Room's cleaner than new snow."

"Hungry, Carl?" Krager eased the van around the snow plows, clearing the parking lot and street in front of St. Swivvens.

"Soup sounds good," Dorn said. "Oatmeal sounds better."

The wind died. Snow filled pot holes along Dodge Street, covered debris: styrofoam, candy and fast food wrappers and cartons, pint and half pint whiskey bottles, and the occasional drunk passed out on the sidewalk.

The Dodge Street Diner, an oblong-shaped, free standing, tan brick building two blocks from the Windsor, had an outside parking lot in front. The lot was empty.

Krager parked in front of the front entrance. They hurried in. The temperature was ten degrees above zero.

They took the booth near the front window and floor space heater.

The waitress had just cleared the table and wiped the coffee and gravy stains. They had the diner to themselves.

"What's the soup like?" Dorn said.

"Wet and hot," the waitress said. "Navy bean and potato. Minestrone."

"How's the oatmeal?"

"We got it naked. Oatmeal. No toppings. We got it with cinnamon. Got it with butter and sugar. Raisins. Shredded apple slices. With cream. Without."

"Great speech." Krager applauded. "Coffee, straight up. Minestrone. Give our senior over here the bill."

Dorn nodded. "Oatmeal. Naked. Tall milk. And the check. Senior discounts?"

"Does this look like a charity arrangement?"

"Actually," Dorn said.

"Well, it ain't. Pay what it says." She flashed a menu which he ignored. "You, darlin'?"

"Hot roast beef sandwich," Kittsy said. "Brown gravy on the mashed. Salad with creamy ranch dressing. Coffee, black."

"Where's all the people?" Krager said.

"Blizzard's comin'."

"Not according to the radio weatherman."

"Live around here for very long you know what the forecaster thinks he knows."

"I lived here most of my life," Pat Krager said. "I get a twinge in the knee before a storm. Ain't twingin' yet."

"When my tail bone starts throbbing it's too late," the waitress said. "Storm's right overhead. Waitin' to drop a load."

"Miss," Dorn said. "We're hungry."

"We wanna beat the crowd," Kittsy said.

"Rush has come and gone. People eating early to get home and out of it before the sky drops."

"How about our eats," Dorn said. "Before the sky drops."

"Sorry, folks. Besides the cook you're the only ones in an hour I can talk to. The cook's too busy picking lottery numbers and he doesn't speak much English." To Krager, she said: "I live a half block east of here. Know the place?"

"The Keen Hotel."

"That's it. I can leave here during a storm and still get home without getting too wet."

"If you want company all I can give ya is a nice tip," Pat said.

"The tip is," Dorn said. "Food. Or we walk."

"Well, if that's how ya feel." She went to the counter. "Hey, Manny, get yer thumb outa yer blow hole. Ordering up. Number One special with coffee. Italian soup. Coffee. Oatmeal, naked, and a tall milk. Oh, and lettuce salad with creamy ranch."

Manny yelled something.

"Comin' right up, folks."

"Miss," Krager said. "After I came back from a state-paid vacation, I stayed at the Keen. Damn near got carried away by the roaches. Big ones. Big as a boxer's fist."

"They spray regularly."

"Who? The roaches?"

"The guys who own the building. Be right back with the drinks."

The clock over the counter read twelve fifteen. Getting dark, the sentry lights vent on. People, head down, hurried into the wind.

The Canadian blow rattled the window, seeped through the plaster walls' cracks.

She brought the drinks on a tray.

"Last time I was in a blizzard," Pat said. "The counter gal ordered us out. Soon as we were, she locked the door, put the closed sign in the window."

"Wasn't very nice." She served the drinks. "Right back with what's next."

She waddled, flat footed, toward the counter.

"She remind you of someone, Carl?" Krager said after a sip.

"Milly."

"Yep."

"Who's Milly?" Kittsy said.

"Someone special," Dorn said.

"A skinhead with a sawed off habit found her behind a convenience store counter," Pat said. "Twenty dollars in the till. Killed her because it wasn't enough."

"Sorry, dear." She went to the ladies room.

The rest of the meal came. The bill was the last item placed on the table.

"Take credit cards?" Dorn said.

"Which ever ya got."

He handed it to her. "In case we need to leave in a hurry."

"We got farther to go than you," Kramer said.

"And I'm wearing running shoes." She plucked the card from the old man's fingers.

Dorn added a milk splash to cool down the oatmeal. Krager sipped coffee, crumbled soda crackers in the soup, mixed and spooned the steaming soup.

"Carl, before she gets back, I need to tell you about her."

Dorn balanced oatmeal on the spoon. "She doesn't give a rat's ring-tone for personal hygiene?"

"I baited her."

"That's what it's called?"

"I prompted her. She opened up about how she feels about certain people."

"How does she feel?"

"Not worth your trust."

"What do you suggest?"

"That snake has two heads. She slithers on her belly real nice. The snake I'm talking about is how I feel about her. She's classier than a souped up stock car, and twice as fast."

Dorn spooned the cereal.

"Where we're going, I don't know if she'd be a help or hindrance."

"We leave her here."

"But I like to pick up what she puts down. I could watch her, do what needs to be done if she becomes a problem."

"She's already a problem."

"Boss, I said some nasty shit at the hotel. She didn't open up until I started talking. Hell, Carl, we live with people who may or may not hate us, for whatever reason. Hell."

"She stays here."

The ladies room door opened.

"Phew," she said, sitting. "I'm ten pounds lighter. How're the eats?"

The waitress brought over Dorn's credit card and the receipt.

"How's everything?" She dragged a hard backed chair from a corner, and sat.

While Dorn added the tip and signed the receipt she massaged her ankles, took the receipt.

"Thanks, folks." She left them.

"Food's good," Kittsy said.

She napkined her chin and mouth.

"Didn't know how hungry I was until I got lip-deep in it."

She belched, a shy, modest sound.

"Bring it up again and we'll vote on it." Pat dropped the spoon in the empty bowl.

"Vote for bloat." She belched, a loud extended noise. She laughed. "Sorry, guys. That's my at-home-alone noise. Don't know where it came from just now."

"The high point of my day," Dorn said over the milk glass's rim.

"We all have one talent," Krager said. "You, Kitts, have two."

"I'd take my bow sitting down, only I'm too busy, gorging on this wonderful stuff." She winked at the old man. "Thanks, Carl."

"Yeah, that's okay."

Pat finished what was in the cup, shook his head when the waitress, coffee pot in hand, approached from behind the counter.

Manny came out, looked through the window. "Ah, madre, madre."

"Now, Manny, it ain't bad as all that."

"Bad enough." He headed for the row of wall pegs behind the counter.

"Out here, hon," the waitress said. "This is nothing. A snow shower is all."

He plucked his thin jacket from the end peg. "You. All-uh you. Finish, okay? We close pretty quick."

At the front door he keyed the lock, propped the "closed" sign in the window.

"You related to a lady who ran a squat and gobble in Lincoln about ten, twelve years ago?" Krager said.

Arms folded, Manny stood by the door, watching them.

Kittsy, sliding across the vinyl covered seat, gulped her coffee.

"Come back again," the waitress said as they made their exit.

XXV

THREE P.M.

Snow began.

By three thirty it filled outside stairwells leading down to dead-bolted warehouse basement doors. Tramps would need other accommodations that night.

The wind.

The narrow ledge outside the hotel's west window was snow-packed to the horizontal frame where the window lock was.

Dorn looked west to the hill leading to the interstate "on" ramp. One car climbed sideways onto the ramp, then slid back down.

Kittsy was in the bathroom. Krager dozed on the bed; pillows propped his head. He awoke suddenly.

"Boss?"

Dorn turned.

"What did you decide? About her?"

"Say your goodbyes."

And then, just then, the bathroom door opened all the way. She charged into the room, red faced, eyes blazing.

"Screw me into the ground, toss me like a used condom."

"I'd pay you off," Dorn said. "With them gone you'd have a life. I gave that to you."

"After I gave them to you." She punched Krager's arm.

He massaged the bicep.

"Move your ass!"

He moved to the bed's far side.

"Move your skinny ass clear across the room!"

He moved to the chair in the corner near the pole lamp.

"I heard your debate."

"Figured you did," the old man said.

She faced Krager. "Dickhead, you sure didn't defend me."

"It's Carl's party."

"At what point did you give away your stones?" The fore-head vein strained. In her throat a pulse beat.

Pat got to his feet.

"Don't you come near me, Slick."

Dorn crossed to the bathroom.

"Carl saved my ass a few years ago. I owe him."

"He owns your ass."

"Call it what you want," Pat said. "Hell, call it freedom."

"What do you call me? A homeless whore?"

"Got your freedom." Dorn turned on the bathroom light. "Or did you enjoy doing it with your brothers?"

Her lips were a pale line across her teeth. Her eyes drilled.

"Rather be a whore than what you are."

Dorn reached under his suit jacket. "What would that be?"

"Killer. Godless excuse for a human being. An excuse who'd never think to save his soul. Oh, I forgot. You don't have a soul." Hands at her sides became fists. "Kike!"

"Oh, Lord." Krager sat.

The wind ceased.

Dorn's hand came out from his suit jacket.

He walked toward the bed. His face was composed.

She stood by the foot; the knee closest to the bed brushed the coverlet.

His fist caught her an inch below the adam's apple. She fell back, caught herself on the inch of exposed mattress, dropped sideways across the bed. Wide, unblinking eyes teared.

"She's your problem, Pat."

He went into the bathroom and closed the door.

After he used and cleaned the catheter, he threw cold water across his face and neck. He patted dry. He tossed the towel in the hamper next to the sink. He waited for the shakes to stop.

When he returned they hadn't moved.

She scowled at him. A bruise covered her throat. Her eyes were red.

Dorn picked up his coat, left the room, shutting the door behind him.

Pat caught him at the elevator. The high ceiling light was one hundred watts, barely illuminating the space in front of the elevator door.

"Want me to do her, Carl?"

Dorn didn't turn. "My job."

He punched the "down" button.

"Sure will miss her," Krager said on the elevator.

"The tenth member of that cell. That's what she is to me. My job, Pat."

In the lobby they dodged passengers just off the bus from Des Moines.

The coffee shop was full. They waited fifteen minutes to be seated. They shared the table with the bus driver.

The driver gestured. "They're evacuees from the flooding over in Iowa. Barely got here. Flood took out the main bridges. Interstate's flooded. Not an acre of good land left for planting. Sorry, men. What me and my passengers been through makes a man want to talk about it."

The waiter dropped menus in front of them. "Food locker's almost empty. Plenty of liquor. Menu's second page."

"What's good?" Krager said.

"Whatever's left."

The driver said, with appropriate hand gesture: "And that would be?"

"Liver and onions, lettuce salad with a tired tomato or two for variety. Creamy ranch dressing or thousand island. Enough booze to float a happy family or three."

They ordered coffee with the liver and onions.

"What do you want on the salad?"

"Surprise me," Dorn said.

"If it's fresh that'll be a surprise."

"Liver tough as a madam's tongue or a beat cop's heels," Dorn said. "Soggy onions. Coffee weaker than I am. When did I end up in Graz. That's in Austria."

"Never had a route through there," the driver said.

Dorn said: "Squat and gobbles every block or so. Food bad as what we're about to eat."

The driver said: "Strictly midwest. Iowa. Nebraska, Wyoming. Idaho. The Dakotas. Where I'm going when I leave here. Idaho."

Krager pushed out of the chair.

A line in front of the men's restroom brought him back to the table.

"Lend me one of those tubes, Carl."

"Only one I have is used."

Pat headed for the lobby.

"Probably piss behind that fake palm near the sign-in desk," the driver said. "I would if I had to go bad enough."

"I have. Many times."

"So, like I was sayin', I've been all over the Midwest. Back and forth. Logged more miles than all the state patrollers put together. Idaho's my favorite. Sparse population. Scenery that's majestic during the warm months. Pretty okay to look at rest of the year. State Department of Roads keep the highways clear. Nice people."

"Know Withersville?"

"Been there a few times. Nice depot. Clean hotel. Called the Motor Inn. Gives over-the-roaders like myself breaks on the rooms," He checked his pocket watch. "Four twenty. Damn. Got to get going." He waved at the waiter. The waiter waved back, continued his conversation with a diner. "Damn, looks like no food for me."

He went over to the waiter. The waiter tabulated the check.

Check in hand, the driver announced; "Folks, the Idaho bus is boarding, soon as I get out there and get the door open. We leave at four thirty. Nine minutes from now."

He led the way into the lobby. He tossed eight food vouchers at the desk clerk.

The five men and three women, gulped coffee, forced down the greasy liver slabs, gagged, choked, rushed through the lobby and out the door.

Krager entered the coffee shop.

"Carl, she's gone."

He got up. "Checked the crapper? Maybe she fell in."

"Don't know where she'd go in this weather."

They checked the street.

The last passenger boarded the bus. Thirty seconds later the bus pulled away from the curb.

"Give her five minutes. She might be back."

"If she isn't?" Pat said.

"We try Hogan's."

Dorn described Kittsy to the desk clerk.

"Yep," he said. "Bought a one-way to Idaho. Left a minute ago."

"Certain it was her?"

"She propositioned me."

"How was she?" Krager said.

"Looked prime. That's as far as it got."

"Grab your coat, Pat. Let's go."

XXVI

MISS LIVER AND ONIONS," Krager said once they passed downtown and entered the interstate's eastern link.

Dorn's hands were folded in his lap. He searched the highway. The salt and sand trucks, behind the snow plows, spread a protective coating. The van was in four-wheel drive.

"Stopping for dinner?" Pat said.

"Breakfast, maybe. When you want a break, yell."

"We spot the bus. Then, what? Force our way on? Drag her off?"

"When we spot the bus we wave it down. One of us gets on before she gets off. Find her. Babysit her."

"On her way to the Withersville rally."

"Good money that's where she's headed. She has contacts there. Her in the equation complicates things. I should've seen what she is. Taken appropriate measures."

"Put a second belly button in her stomach."

"I was thinking about her forehead. A jacket right above the bridge."

"I should've screwed her silly and dropped her somewhere, thanking God for good lovers."

"She screwed us both silly. Incest victims can tell me anything and I'll believe it."

Krager tapped the brake. A black pickup with Wyoming plates pulled off a side road, cut in front of the van.

A gun rack was mounted above the cab's back window. A confederate flag, attached to the driver's side mirror, was wind whipped.

Krager used the horn. "Nebraska drivers are bad. Wyoming jockeys are worse."

"I'd feel better if we could do it without it looking like a kidnapping," Dorn said.

"Torch the bus."

"What if she's not on the bus?"

"She bought a ticket."

"A diversion?" Dorn sighed.

"Maybe."

Dorn flinched. "My bladder feels like a seal has slapped it with its tail."

"Makes you wanna honk, huh?"

"Next shoulder, pull over."

"Right up ahead."

Beyond the shoulder was the Idaho bound bus.

"There it is. What do we do?"

"Catch the bus later. Right now, I got a medical emergency."

The bus turned toward the Wyoming border, disappeared in wind driven snow showers.

Dorn got out, turned away from the van.

Bladder empty, he shivered, rubbed his hands.

"Icicles hanging from my jerk-stick."

"If the weather gets worse they might shack up somewhere. Like we should do."

"Okay."

Krager pressed the accelerator.

The Idaho bus was parked in a motel lot a half mile down the interstate.

Krager pulled in.

The black pickup with the gun rack pulled out ahead of them.

The bus driver was in the lobby, passing travel vouchers across the reception desk. Through the side window Dorn searched for her. Passengers entered their rooms.

The driver looked up from the tickets in his hands. "Hey, aren't you two . . ."

"All two of us," Dorn said.

"Say, isn't this weather nasty?"

"Your last pick up?"

"The lady back at the hotel. She's not with us."

"She's dead?" Krager took a blunt from its case.

The clerk cleared his throat, gestured at the "no smoking" sign. The sign was above the desk.

"Far as I know, she's not," the driver said. "Got picked up by a pickup with four wheel drive, snow tires and a husky farm boy."

Krager, by the door, looked out. "No pickups."

"They pulled out thirty, forty seconds ago."

"Boss, I gotta eat."

The coffee shop was across the lobby.

"Get it to go, Pat."

XXVII

SIX P.M.

The snow stopped.

No traffic ahead or behind the van.

Dorn drove. The arsonist dozed. Dorn turned on the radio. Static. They skirted the Sidney, Nebraska city limits, exited Nebraska, crossed into Wyoming.

The sentry lights barely cut the shadows of the surrounding mountains; the shadows thickened. The headlights showed what was in front of the high beams. And that's all.

The dashboard light illuminated their knees.

The static cleared.

"This is KWYO, your fifty thousand watt friend in Cheyenne, Wyoming. Snow and blowing snow with below zero temperatures are expected in Wyoming and western Nebraska, through tomorrow. Periods of freezing rain should accompany the snow through tomorrow. Temps should drop to ten below after dark. Expect a high tomorrow of ten to fifteen above. Expected snow accumulations: two to four inches by sundown tomorrow. Take heart, dear heart. Warmer weather's on the way. By April Fools Day. Five more months."

"Smart fuck." Dorn turned off the radio.

"Bad ass weather," Krager said, eyes closed.

"I can drive through this. Can't I?"

"Keep it at forty miles per. Above that's chancy."

"Withersville's four hundred miles northwest."

"Four tanks'll get us there."

"Van got the grunts to get us there?"

Pat gave a sideways glance. "Not worried about the van."

"Hate's a strong mood gooser."

"We all need something." Krager turned on his side, facing the passenger's door.

"Stretch it in back."

"I'm okay, boss."

"Okay."

Dorn guided the van around frozen snow clumps. Under the snow was black ice: hidden ice, treacherous to drivers as a greased wire is to aerialists.

Pat sniffed. "One of us smells like spoiled milk."

"New aftershave."

"Nobody's perfect."

Dorn yawned.

"Don't." Pat sat up.

"Torrington's ahead. Ninety miles."

"Steak houses up the wazoo, if memory serves."

"From Torrington it's six hundred miles."

"Did a job outside Torrington. When the bottom dropped out of the real estate market, this developer dropped a dime and I met him in Grand Island, Nebraska. Over steaks we made the deal. Him, his investors and yours truly did well on the deal."

"How did he know where to find you?"

"Like you found me. Through my agent."

"Vince Hallsted."

"That's the man."

"Sifted a ton of ash before I discovered his DNA. He used a special mix. I traced the chemist who supplied the works. From the chemist to Hallsted's crib. Caught him doing a mix. Before he torched himself he was a friend."

"Put a few dollars in his pocket?"

Dorn nodded. "How's he doing?"

"He's doing. That last job in seventy-five cost him his legs. He keeps me and three other guys working."

"The Kanesville job?"

"That was his."

"He ID the client?"

"Not to me."

"Tell him I said hi."

"Sure will." Krager, yawning and stretching, tapped the dash's underside with his knees.

"How're the motels?"

"Nice motel. On the ashes of the old. Friendly price. Was, anyway."

"Eight hours down time sound good?"

Eyes shut, Pat raised an index finger.

XXVIII

HOLIDAY LIGHTS BLINKED.

The curb-side snow banks along Torrington's seven block main street turned red, black, red, black, as rhythmic as a railroad crossing signal.

Dorn rolled down the window, gulped clean air. "Where's the food?"

"Where the motel is."

Pat gave directions.

Seven P.M. and the street was deserted. The van cut tire tracks in the snow. Store windows on both sides of the street displayed pre-holiday sale items. Otherwise, the stores were dark.

Music came from around the corner at street's end. The tavern's "welcome" sign drilled darkness surrounding the twin story brick building.

A man staggered out, straightened, started for the pickup parked on a snow bank at the curb in front of the tavern.

Dorn tapped the brakes, cruised past.

The man, fumbling with a key ring, was bent, scrawny, almost lost in the knee-length coat.

Dorn pulled in front of the pickup just as the driver dropped the keys. Dorn got out.

The man looked bewildered, head swinging side to side while he tried to focus on the snow bank, where the keys fell.

"Help you?" Dorn said.

The man looked, steadied himself against the door. "Damn keys."

"Saw where you dropped them. Here, let me help."

"Anything you can do, brother." The driver vomited in the street. Wiping his chin, he said: "When you pay fifty cents for a bar whiskey double what do you expect?"

"Liver disease." Dorn groped around the spot where he thought the keys were. "Ah, here they are."

He shook the key ring. Snow wisps scattered like dust-devils under foot.

"Damn, brother, permit me to buy you a drink."

"Need to find a buddy. Do you know . . ."

"Know everybody here. All four hundred of 'em."

"Drives a black pickup." He described it.

"Sounds like Neal Cardozi's wagon. Lives two miles west of here on the other side of the train tracks. Under a lotta trees which is how he likes it. Secluded, you know."

"I think I do."

XXIX

THE ONE ROOM wood frame shack was sheltered by an oak grove. One window in front wide enough for one person to look out of. Light shone beneath the rough muslin drape's hem.

When the van pulled off the road, onto a shoveled two-lane macadam drive and stopped near the front door, a face appeared at the window.

Krager waved.

The drapes closed.

The door opened.

A scrawny old man in bib overalls, flannel shirt and boots stood in the doorway. The muzzle of his double barreled shotgun was pointed at Carl Dorn.

"Git off'n my property," he said in a high, old man's quavery voice. His aim was steady.

Dorn and Krager didn't move.

"Looking for my granddaughter," Dorn said. "Might be traveling with Neal Cardozi. Is he here?"

"Was here." He spread his legs for balance. "Left five, ten minutes ago. What you want him for?"

"Passing through," Krager said. "On our way to Withersville, Idaho."

Dorn said: "Decided to make the Idaho trip after all. After she left. Wanted to catch up with her."

"Stayed long enough to slip it to her, pack a bag, and goodbye. Left a mess for me to clean up."

"What mess?" Pat said.

"Woman's mess, you know."

"Haven't known in a long time," Carl said. "Which way did they go?"

"Only one way." He put down the gun. "Across the tracks down there, turn right, onto the interstate. That's a good mile from here. Keep on the interstate until the Idaho border. This side of the border is a lodge at the bottom of the Grand Teton range. State owned and marked by signs. So unless you're asleep, you can't miss it. Neal shacks up there when he's romancing a broad. Teton Lodge's the name. Drive careful now. Roads to the interstate are icy."

He slammed, double bolted the door.

" 'Bout froze my man-gland," Pat said in the driver's seat.

"Too tired to feel anything."

"I'd sing ya a lullaby. Might put myself to sleep."

"Don't need no lullabies."

Dorn snored.

"Guess you don't."

Three hundred fifty miles later, around seven A.M. Krager took the interstate exit to a semi-circular access road, up an incline, onto the highway. He followed the signs to the Teton Lodge, a four story, granite and log wood structure, styled like a ranch house. It was a mile east of the Teton Range.

Dorn stumbled in, behind Krager.

They yawned through the lengthy registration.

The garage was in back, under the cement sign that read: "Garage."

"After I park it, Carl, I'm going for breakfast."

"We have a complimentary breakfast buffet." The clerk put two tickets on the desk.

Dorn gave Krager his ticket. "He's eating for two," Dorn told the clerk.

The smile hurt the old man's cheeks.

"Knock on my door around noon, Pat. If you're up."

"I will be."

Dorn left him in the lobby.

In his room, he threw cold water on his face and neck.

He used the catheter.

After consulting a paper slip from his wallet, he used the phone.

"Hallsted residence," a child singsonged.

"Kenya, this is Uncle Carl. Remember me?"

"Uh . . . no."

"Is your dad at home?"

"He's always at home. Wanna talk to him?"

"Yes."

"Daddy!"

A pause. Then: "Who is this?"

"Carl Dorn."

A muffled laugh.

"Haven't thought of you since I cashed that last check."

"Got another one with your name on it."

"Who needs incinerating?"

"I need to know who Pat Krager's client was, the one who had him torch Kanesville, Iowa."

"He torched the town?" Hallsted's voice cracked.

"Only what the client wanted. Who was it?"

"Confidential, Carl."

Dorn named a figure. "That open any closed files?"

"Well . . ."

"Money's in the bank, Vince. Tell me now, I write the check now and it goes out in the noon mail."

A pause.

"Nobody knows I'm telling you."

"No one will know."

Vince said a name.

Dorn frowned. "Thought so. Thanks. Still at seven seventeen Laurel Canyon Road?"

"Too poor to move."

Dorn wrote the check, found an envelope and stamp, tucked the envelope in the jacket's inside pocket.

He lay on the bed, shoes off, stared at his toes visible through the frayed wool, stared at the reflections on the ceiling.

The drapes wouldn't completely close. Colors flashed.

He tried to sleep.

When Pat knocked on the door, the old man was still awake.

He opened the door.

Pat came in, went to the armchair across from the door.

"Put on your shoes, boss. Lunch is being served."

"Any trace . . ."

"None. Waitress in the coffee shop thought Cardozi and Kittsy were in earlier. They ate like they'd never eaten before. Then they took off. I talked with the desk clerk. Cardozi signed in using his real name and credit card. Their room was three-one-one. Vacant now."

The elevator arrived. On the way down neither spoke. Dorn counted stains on the carpet. Krager yawned, scratched his butt.

In the lobby, as they crossed to the coffee shop, Dorn said:

"Six hundred miles to go. If the weather cooperates, we could be there in seventy-two hours."

"Up to it?"

They took a booth.

"Have to be," Dorn said. "Getting there is the easy part. The fun part's when we go to work."

The waitress came over.

They ordered beef stew with hot butter beans, lettuce salad with Italian dressing. Milk for the old man. Coffee for his partner.

"Don't want you pooping out on me," Krager said. "Couldn't give you a decent funeral. No money."

"Born poor. Die poor. Worse than that out there."

"Always is."

The meal arrived. They ate, avoided eye contact. Pat cleared his throat. Dorn ignored him. The check came. The old man examined it, brought out his credit card.

"Pony time," he said. "Then we go."

Dorn paid the check, left Krager with a coffee refill. He used the mail drop-box next to the elevator.

Krager read the local newspaper in a wing chair in the lobby.

"I'll drive," the elderly man said.

Krager climbed in back. "Sure you're up to this, Carl?"

"I'm fine." Dorn eased the van out of the garage, up a ramp to the road that took them to the interstate.

"Wake me if you feel it," Krager said.

"At first yawn you'll know."

"Make it the second one. I need time to wake up."

The sky was overcast. Wind at a steady twenty miles from the north. The interstate was plowed and sanded. With little traffic.

"No new snow to report," the radio weatherman said. "None expected for the next twenty-four hours."

They left the Tetons. The radio signal faded. Dorn adjusted the dial setting.

"This is KIFI-AM, with the tall tower and lots of power, Idaho Falls, Idaho. This half hour of easy listening brought to you by the Easy Time Inn off the Wydaho Road, just north of interstate forty-six."

"Sounds like fun," Krager said in Dorn's ear.

"Dammit, Pat. Almost made me bomb my bloomers."

"Boss, I been watching you weave from one lane to the other. Before you kill us, pull over."

Dorn thought, said: "Guess so. We have time."

"If they start their goose-stepping before we get there, we'll demand a rerun."

Dorn lowered the window. After he was wind cooled and teary eyed he rolled it up.

"Carl, right over there."

Dorn pulled out of the outside lane, onto the shoulder.

In the passenger's seat the retired arson cop fell asleep. "Carl, we're here."

"Where?"

"Easy Time Inn."

Dorn slept till five. Krager's knock woke him.

"Up for oatmeal, or something more thrilling?"

The arsonist had showered and changed clothes. The pepper smell was in his pores and came out with the sweat. Aftershave and deodorant couldn't kill the stink.

"A shower first," Dorn said. "See you downstairs."

He met Pat in the lobby. The early evening rush hadn't begun. They had a choice: table or booth. The table they chose came with a view.

The Snake River, directly below, glinted in the deepening sunset. Two fishermen hunkered over a hole in the ice. Their lines remained motionless.

"Too cold for the fish, even," Dorn said.

"Not too cold for fools," Krager said. "Man, I'd have to be trolling for gold to sit on a box on a river in below zero weather."

"I eat fish."

"Same. Long as they can't eat me first."

The TV over the counter was on. In the middle of a gas-bag get-together, the screen went to white. The title card, covering the screen, read: "Special Report."

The news reader came on: "This just in. Idaho Falls oldest synagogue, and a nearby Catholic Church were destroyed this afternoon. No one injured. Damage estimated in the millions. Rabbi David Greenberg tells channel four that moments before the blast that engulfed the one-hundred year old house of worship, he received a call, warning of the impending explosion. No claims of responsibility have been received by police or the media. Stay tuned to channel four for updates. Repeating . . ."

The waitress switched stations. The game show: *Beat Your Wife* was on.

Dorn looked away from the menu. Krager peered at him over the menu's rim.

"Must have been a gas leak," the younger man said.

"The utility company made the call?"

"Well, if you put it that way . . ." An open handed gesture.

The waitress stood behind Krager, faced Dorn, gave the old man a cheek dimpling smile.

"Polish dog with kraut," Dorn said. "No mustard. No ketchup. Potato cakes if they're not greasy."

"Drier than a dead man's eyes." She bit her lip. Her eyes teared. She blushed but held back the laugh.

The men ignored her.

"Soup of the day, whatever it is." Dorn closed the menu.

"Tomato and rice."

"Tea with lemon."

"Only way to drink it. You, sir?"

Krager said: "Fried pork steak. Scalloped potatoes. Whatever vegetable you have."

"Stewed tomatoes and cucumbers."

"House dressing on the salad."

"Thousand Island or French?"

"Surprise me."

"And to drink?"

"Coffee. Blacker than ice on a road."

"Bread?"

"Not for me," Dorn said.

"Don't you serve bread as part of the meal?"

"Only if the customer asks. Grain shortage, you know."

"Didn't know," Pat said.

"We have plain wheat, or white, or cottage white, or potato bread or, for an additional ninety nine cents, assorted breads in a nice sampler basket."

"Forget the bread," Pat said.

"Forgotten."

She took their menus.

The ice fishermen spooled their lines, picked up their boxes, picked their way across the ice to the shore.

Dorn steepled his fingers, watched a roach rush across the buffed floor.

"While you were counting ZZZZs, I asked questions, walked to the business district about three, four blocks from here, asked more questions, eyeballed every pickup truck parked or passing. Like she and her John don't exist."

Soup, salads and drinks arrived.

When she returned to the kitchen, Dorn said: "Heard any updated forecasts?"

"More cold. No snow." Krager added pepper to the lettuce and tomatoes. "Not enough sun to light the inside of a thimble. Something on your mind?"

"Anxious."

"Need to finish this, pardon the obvious."

"Don't know if I can make it. A slip on the ice. An interruption of my focus. An unexpected bit of bad news. That'll throw me."

"Stay focused. Watch where you throw your feet. Ignore the news."

"Some news you can't ignore."

"Carl, I'm not you. Riddles confuse me."

"On the job, I solved them with help. Find clues. Bits of charred wood. Pieces of ember so fragile I needed a tweezer to fill a cellophane bag. I turned over the debris to the microscope squinters. They discovered the secrets, and the solutions. I reached conclusions based on what the lab people told me. No lab advisors now."

"What're we talking about?"

"Coincidence?"

"Church and synagogue here? Same in Kanesville?"

"Coincidence."

The waitress brought the entrees.

"Barely touched your soup, and. Salad okay? Soup?"

"Good," Dorn said.

"We were distracted," Krager said. "Two men. Ice fishing."

"Ten degrees warmer and it'd be short-sleeve-shirt fishing. Got to be rugged, men, to survive in this climate."

"We're passing through," the old man said.

"Passing through and trying not to pass out from the cold," Pat said.

"Bring the check any time," Dorn said.

"Coming right up." She waved to the ice fishermen. They sat at a table by the lobby door. They waved back.

"Who won, guys? You or the fish?"

Dorn frowned. "Perkiness is like a barking damn dog at three A.M. Two feet from my crib."

"Think I did the torch job while you slept?"

"I didn't sleep much."

"Copycat crimes, Carl. Closer to Withersville the number of copycats will increase. What I did in Kanesville was not a hate crime. Forgive me for earning a living and creating a mini trend."

He attacked the pork.

XXXI

A T MIDNIGHT they got in the van. At ten next morning they crossed the Salmon River. Three hundred miles north of the river was the small town of Lewiston. North of Lewiston: Coeur D'Alene and farther north a smaller town eight miles from the Canadian border: Withersville, Idaho.

The interstate was clear. North-South traffic moderate. A sunny thirty-two degrees.

Krager drove. "The snow must have gone south without stopping here."

Dorn cleaned the thirty-eight. "Got to stop in Lewiston."

"Got friends there?"

"Not unless you consider indoor plumbing friends."

Krager nodded. "I could damp down an inferno with what I'm holding."

On Lewiston's southern border there was a store front gambling hall. The boast on the front window: "Easiest slots in the state."

Behind the store front was a two story tan brick motel.

One vehicle in the open parking lot and it was a black pickup.

"The piss can wait," Dorn said.

An old man played the slots, three machines at a time. The bartender, behind the counter, dozed on a hardbacked chair.

"Yeah," the bartender said when Dorn tickled her nose with a twenty dollar bill, "I'm desk clerk, too. Room seven."

She turned the register toward Dorn.

"Cardozi and wife" on the top line. Credit card payment. "We don't have many guests this time of year. Sun Valley way south of here gets the trade."

"Where's the closest fill-er-up?" Krager said.

"Gregg's Gasatorium. Mile north down the road."

Outside, Krager fired up a blunt. He smoked it while he squinted at passing traffic. Dorn held an unlighted cigar, looked at it, put it back in the cigar case.

"They're alone," Dorn said.

"Unless they're not."

"My chance. The one I have to take. Wait outside. Unless you need to slip it in one last time."

"Be the first free-bee I got off a whore."

"Free stuff's what costs the most."

"How do you get in?"

"Knock and step to one side."

"Pops, you're talking like an amateur. Got a tool in the van that's better than a door key."

Krager brought out an iron shaft with a hand grip and a handle midway down the shaft and, at the end, a steel ball.

A final puff. He flicked the stub into the gutter.

Room seven was on the east end, first floor. A ragged bush guarded the door.

Dorn held the thirty-eight at his side.

Krager swung the weapon straight back, then forward. It splintered wood above the knob.

The door flew open, banged against the wall.

The radio blared.

Cardozi sat in the arm chair across from the door. He dropped the German language newspaper, leaped to his feet. He wore jockeys and an undershirt. His biceps were tattooed with swastikas.

Shrieking, he threw himself at the lamp table near the bed. Before he reached the snub-nosed revolver on the table, he twisted his ankle, stumbled. Arms waving, he fell.

Cursing, screaming, he slammed his right knee against the concrete floor. His knee bled. He crawled toward the table.

His fingers grubbled space.

He wept, rolled on his side, facing the old man. Arms outstretched, he posted a barrier of palms.

Dorn raised his arm. Exhaled, took a breath, held it.

"Where's the cunt?" Pat said.

He stood next to Dorn.

"Bath . . . bathroom . . . uh . . ."

The neo-Nazi's eyelids fluttered. A stain appeared on the front of his briefs.

"Say hello to Hitler." Dorn put a pair, one above the other, in Cardozi's forehead, directly above the bridge of his flat nose.

Cardozi jerked, rolled to the bed. An arm lifted, fell. The room stank of his last meal.

Krager tapped the bathroom door.

"Oh, Kittsy," he singsonged. "Your future's here."

Nothing.

"Let me." Dorn reloaded. He put the chamber's load across the door, left to right, at belly level.

Except for the echo no other sound.

Dorn nodded. Krager slammed the door. Balanced on one hinge, it sagged into the room. Dorn reloaded. Krager stepped over the door, checked the shower, the utility closet.

He said: "She ain't here."

They went out.

The pickup burned rubber in a U-turn.

Dorn fired, clipped the metal bridge next to the rear exhaust.

The bartender came out. The pickup weaved onto the road, turned north.

"Damn glad they paid up front," the bartender said.

Pat reached the van first. He had the van in motion, stopped in front of the elderly man. Dorn reached for the door handle.

"Gas gauge is red-lining." Krager pointed the van north. "With his last breath that sonofabitch lied to us."

"What do you expect from a Nazi? With the rope around their necks they'd give the sieg heil."

"Catch on quick."

XXXII

WHILE KRAGER filled the van's tank, Dorn drained his.

"Seen a black pickup with Wyoming plates, heading north?" Pat said.

"Nope," the attendant said. "Not today anyway."

"Interstate access straight ahead?"

"Straight ahead."

On the interstate they stayed in the outside northbound lane.

"I never tried their bathroom door, Carl."

"Wouldn't have saved time. While I put that Nazi in a more deserving place she was probably at the ice machine or the condom dispenser. She had a good start before you kicked in the bathroom door. I hope she doesn't have a cell phone."

"Who would she call? The psychic hotline?"

The old man's face was expressionless.

"Oh?" Krager said. "Maybe we should turn back."

"We're too close."

"I'm too young to die."

"I know how to use your rig."

"Do you know where the target is?"

Dorn showed the one sheet taken from the Kanesville tramp.

"The meeting place? A stone castle? A single story wood frame with oak and elm for neighbors?"

"We'll find out. If you can't do it, we leave."

A mile, and fifteen minutes later, Krager smiled.

"She's a survivor. Knew we were coming. Got his keys."

"Luck ends. Real sudden. It did for him."

One hundred miles later, at three P.M., they entered Coeur D'Alene, drove the main street.

"There it is." Krager said.

"Parked there like she has all the time there is."

Krager parked at the curb, a block away. The pickup was empty. The hood was warm.

"I can smell her," Dorn said.

"I can't smell anything." Pat reached for his handkerchief. "Haven't blown my nose today."

The block was newly painted one story frame buildings. Each business was free standing and housed one business each. Narrow space separated each from its neighbor.

Two taverns, one on the north corner, the other on the south, faced. A movie theater in the middle of the block with the sheriff's office next to it.

"She's not with the sheriff," Dorn said.

"Never know who she's selling it to."

They canvassed both sides of the street.

The pickup was locked and empty.

Krager said: "In the mood for a movie?"

The film was a low budget action film: *Tuxedo Square Job.*

"Why not?"

"I'll pop for the popcorn."

Inside the hundred seat theater the old man filled his hand with the thirty-eight.

"Your eyes are better than mine," Kramer said.

But they each took an aisle.

The elderly woman midway in row four sucked on a straw. It was imbedded in a tall iced coffee.

The woman in the first row wasn't Kittsy, either.

They turned to go.

The side exit opened. The late afternoon sun showed their target. She hurried out. They hurried after her.

Outside, in the space between buildings, Krager went one way; Dorn the other.

The old arson cop stepped over empty beer and whiskey bottles, used condoms, partially gnawed chicken and rib bones.

She was across the street. A few more feet and she would reach the truck. Gasping, he dodged traffic, to the side of the street she was on.

She was in the truck, fumbling with the ignition key.

Dorn pressed the thirty-eight's muzzle against the driver's window.

He formed the command: "Out."

The door opened.

The elderly man faced the shotgun's business end.

He put a slug in the ceiling above her head. Metal chips showered. She dropped the gun, knuckled her eyes, partially blinded by the flash and falling debris.

Holding the shot gun's barrel, Dorn slammed the butt into her jaw.

She cried out, fell back, whimpering, holding a cupped palm to her dripping lower lip.

"Glad to see you, too," Dorn said.

Krager came over. "Our wandering Nazi."

Stunned, she dribbled blood, said nothing.

They escorted her to the van.

XXXIII

ORN DROVE.

  Pat was in back with their prisoner.

  She slept.

When Dorn left the interstate for a dirt road she woke up.

He parked beside a drainage ditch, under a fifty foot elm.

The early evening moon penetrated the clenched branches. Light slivers dotted their faces. They stood on the ditch edge.

"Rape me first?" she said.

"Selling at a discount?" Krager said.

"I called Nauman. Just before you butchered Cardozi. They will be waiting. A shame I won't be there, cheering them on."

"You, my dear, will see them soon enough." The old man stepped back.

Krager started for the van.

Eyes glinting, she growled: "Jew . . ."

Three rapid shots punctured her forehead, her right eye, her throat under the adam's apple, adding bright red to the scarlet and black of their last encounter.

Arms flailing, she toppled. The dead weight's thump hitting weed-choked mud brought him to the ditch's rim. He fired twice.

In the driver's seat, Pat puffed on a blunt.

"So we're going to certain death," he said. "That how it shakes for you?"

"I'm nearly there."

"I'm not."

"Drop me in Withersville."

"I need the money."

"Skinheads won't give us exit choices. We won't, either. That's the guarantee, pal."

"Never met a guarantee I didn't like."

"Can't like this one. All I can promise."

Withersville was eight miles north of Coeur D'Alene. The north end faced wide sidewalks and were flanked by fifty-year-old oak and ash. The smallest house was two stories and woodframe. The others were three stories with broad porches and barred front doors. Cadillacs and Rolls were parked in back, at the top of wide, winding driveways.

Signs at the curb directed them to the South Street bus depot. Krager parked in the side lot. He walked the lobby while Dorn used the mens room. When Dorn came out, Krager showed him a handbill.

"Blonde chick over there pushed this on me," he said, outside.

"Rally tonight. Seven o'clock. Nauman compound. Ten-Eleven Delaware Road," it read.

A map showed how to get there.

XXXIV

THEY DROVE through the town square. At the east end, they turned right.

Ten Eleven Delaware Road was on the hill, overlooking the town. It was at the east end of the street, facing south. Withersville was an oblong, extending from the hill, to the south and north.

Emil Nauman's compound was a two-story stone castle with a turret, high stone walls and an iron front gate. Sentry lights illuminated the courtyard. Lights on both floors were muted behind thick, velvet drapes.

"Cozy, no?" Pat lip chewed.

Dorn grunted.

Behind them, two pickups waited.

A man with a rifle came through the narrow door beside the gate. Krager showed the handbill. Showed phony ID. The man nodded. The gate opened.

The man pointed to the winding drive and the main entrance.

Behind the house was the smaller carriage house. Lights there were at their lowest settings.

Two men, rifles slung on their shoulders, waved them down, demanded IDs.

"Okay." He handed back Krager's phony ID card.

The other squinted at Dorn's. "Torgolson. What kind-uh name's Torgolson?"

"Norwegian."

He took another look. "Yeah, I'm dark-Norse myself."

He pointed.

Krager parked at the far end of the driveway, facing Delaware Road. He strapped on a shoulder holster, loaded a three-fifty-seven Magnum, secured the holster and its contents.

"Feels like I got a bull's leg attached to my chest."

He got out.

Dorn was at his side.

Four cement steps to the open front door. Between them and the door were two armed guards.

"Hey," when a guard recognized the bulge under Pat's jacket.

He frisked, found the Magnum.

"Protection, man. Against some homicidal minority person who might get past you."

"Shit." The second guard spat tobacco juice. "Twenty armed men. We worked for Blackwater in Iraq. We're on both floors. We can handle it."

"Don't need no amateur, packing heat. Take it off."

Pat unbuckled the holster.

"Gel it back on your way out." He took it, put it in a box on the floor, at the end of a row of boxes.

"Box number eleven," the second guard said.

"When the speechifying begins, the boxes will be locked."

While this exchange was going on Dorn casually distanced himself from Krager, entered, examined the oil paintings on the walls.

Scenes of battles and pillaging.

Wagner's *Ride of the Valkyries* played at low volume while a young man in uniform photographed everyone who entered.

"For Herr Nauman's scrapbook," he told everyone.

Across front the front entrance was a staircase. On the stair landing an oil of a young Emil Nauman in uniform.

Dorn winced.

The portrait, lifelike in every detail, flashbacked Dorn to Dachau.

He rubbed his eyes. His fingertips were damp.

Another oil was next to the elder Nauman's portrait. The subject was a fat-faced middle aged man, with thick short blond hair, piercing blue eyes, thick cheekbones and lips.

This had to be Forslund Nauman, the old Nazi's son.

Krager entered the front hall. One of the guards followed. Inside, Krager offered a blunt and when both cigars were lit, the arsonist engaged the guard in conversation.

Dorn found a door at the rear of the hall, near the staircase. Into the kitchen and up a narrow staircase in the pantry.

A dim light at the top of the stairs guided him to the second floor and through another door into a long hall.

He stopped for breath.

He heard from the floor below: "Good evening. Many of you know me. For those who don't, I'm Forslund Nauman. Emil, our leader, is my Fuhrer and my father. I look around, see six determined, concerned citizens. And I recall something father said: It's not the number of men who win wars, it's the dedication of the few who choose to follow. Only six tonight. If you truly are ready to give of yourselves then you have the strength of six hundred. My . . . our Fuhrer wishes he could be here to welcome you, enjoy your company, share his many stories that, hopefully, will guide you in our noble task. Unfortunately, father is in frail health. But when he talks about our glory days he is young, vigorous, full of the promise of our fatherland, the Aryan race, and the man who directed us for too short a time in our righteous pursuits. I'm speaking, of course, of our Fuhrer. His dedication is a beacon for all who choose to follow."

Mutterings, followed by: "yes, yes" from Krager.

"I will speak with each of you, in private. After, we will discuss our plans. During these interviews the rest of you may enjoy the comfort of a warm fire. Which, I have to say, is what the future holds for those who oppose what we stand for."

A scuffling of feet, of chairs.

"Down the hall, there. I will be with you shortly."

Dorn held the thirty-eight at his side.

Two doors, down the hall, faced. At the first door he pressed an ear to the smooth, cool oak surface. A respirator rhythmically wheezed.

His hand was on the door knob when:

"Stop right there," from behind him.

XXXV

DORN WAS RELIEVED of the thirty-eight, frisked, guided down the back stairs and out the kitchen door, to the carriage house.

Inside, two men in suits smoked, watched closed circuit TV.

"Got the star of our show without a problem?" A short, fat man with a big neck and small head gave Dorn the up and down.

He forced himself out of the swivel chair, came over, flashed his ID. The badge was an FBI silver shield. The ID's photo matched the sweating, porcine face.

The agent's name was William Sowers.

He wore a bank president's navy blue suit, white shirt, black tie, black custom-made shoes.

He had the breath of a homeless wino.

According to his ID he was forty-eight.

The second man seated in front of the TV screens got up, pushed the chair toward Dorn.

"Sit," Agent Sowers said.

Dorn sat.

After filling out a short report form, Dorn's escort exited.

"On the job a hundred percent," Dorn said.

"We were notified. Some broad said you'd make an appearance and here you are, as promised. Not all broads are liars."

He blushed.

"That's what friends are for," Dorn said.

"Like being in one of those concentration camps. Betrayal for a bread crust."

"Sorry to say, yes."

Agent Sowers handkerchiefed his flushed, veined cheeks and forehead.

The second agent went out, saying: "Call me when you're finished."

"Ball busting? I'm four feet from the bone yard. So bust away."

"If I need to."

Sowers pushed his chair closer. They were knee to knee.

"Don't know what I'd do if I'd been in one." He gave Dorn a damp eyed look, then looked away. "Much as I like booze, don't think I could have survived. But sympathy buys nothing at the grocery and liquor stores. I won't waste any on you. Got ID? Not that phony shit you showed at the door."

"Which one was yours?"

"More than one."

Dorn showed what was in his wallet.

"Arson cop. Retired. Funny line of work after what you been through. Ya see when I got your name from the broad I looked you up. The picture on the law enforcement website was an old one. Had to make sure you were the right guy."

Dorn nodded.

"Glad you're letting me do the chin music. Makes the routine faster."

"Late date?"

"With a jug of Canadian Club. My nickname's whiskey."

"Whiskey sours?"

He nodded, spilling perspiration across Dorn's cheeks.

"Got the name during my academy days. Because I enjoy it so much. The academy. The booze after a long day. Women betray you. Booze never does." He sat back. "Yeah, I really love it."

"Mine's Nazi killer. For the same reason."

"Which dovetails into what you gotta know. No Nazi kills here. Not the old man. Yeah, we know what he was, and still is. In 1946 we needed what he knew and he gave us all kinds of nifty weapons. Terrible instruments that the public never knew about. We used terrible things on our enemies, beginning with the Russians. So, for faithful service to this country, he got his citizenship and a live till he dies guarantee from us. The kid's another story. And a short story at that. Put him in a pine box and throw on the dirt for all I give a rat's ass. Burn the house. Just don't fuck with the old man."

"If Emil dies of natural causes?"

"A pillow over the face isn't natural causes."

"If he stops breathing without help."

"Make sure it happens when you're nowhere near, and have alibis."

Dorn pushed out of the chair. "Thanks for the warning."

"Hold it."

"I'm trying to."

"Wait a minute. Not done here."

"I got to walk my widdle. Drain the third leg."

"Pissatorium's right over there."

When Dorn came back the agent had a whiskey glass tilted to his breadloaf-sized lips.

"Ah." He licked his lips. "Can't beat the blend. Canada gave the world resort-like summers and the best whiskey. I'd offer you some but less for you, more for me. Yep, we ought to make Canada one of ours. Like we did Alaska."

"Don't think that would play anywhere north of here."

"Suppose not. Over there on the table's a blank tablet and ball point. Bring it over, will ya? Hate to spoil the mood by moving. Oh, on that other table's a Polaroid Land camera. Bring that, too, will ya?"

When Dorn was seated, Sowers dictated: "I, Carl Dorn, have been advised by Special Agent in charge William Sowers that if I attempt to harm Emil Nauman, who resides at Ten Eleven Delaware Road, Withersville, Idaho, I will be held accountable for my actions. Further, I agree not to hinder the FBI in its round the clock protection of said Nauman. If I violate the terms of this contract I can expect swift and severe punishment by the FBI. Signed this date: November 28, 2008."

Sowers aimed the camera.

"Sign it. Now turn the tablet toward me."

A pause while the photos developed.

"Old as it is, it takes a super-sharp picture. Okay, Mr. Dorn. Our business is done. Except for one more question. Where's your co-conspirator?"

"He bugged out on me."

"Now that's not so. We have you both entering. Now where is he?"

"We separated. Don't know where he is."

"Man, this just isn't your night."

"Never is."

"This is your chance to walk away. Where the hell is he?"

"Let me look."

"Like hell." He forced the cell phone from his jacket pocket.

"Okosi, we got an intruder. Tall, skinny, late middle age. Dressed casual, like a billing clerk in an insurance company who doesn't care how he looks. On the grounds or in the main house. No, don't alert the Blackwater troops. Our intrusion. Our problem. No, he isn't armed." He turned toward Dorn. "Is he?"

XXXVI

SOWERS SAID into the cell phone: "Hold yer water. I'm comin'."

He lumbered out the door, leaving Dorn and Dorn's thirty-eight,

The weapon lay on a table, on a paper pile.

Seven P.M.

Dorn dragged himself outside. The air, this close to the border, was crisp, smelled of the nearby pine forests.

A clear sky. The moon yet to rise.

He tried the kitchen door.

Unlocked.

Two skinheads sat at the table, sipping coffee. Their M-16 rifles leaned against the wall behind them, within reach.

The door opened.

The squeak raised their eyes.

They didn't see the steel jackets coming, looked surprised when they arrived.

The echo momentarily deafened the old man.

He grabbed a rifle. Lightweight, easy for an old man to fire.

Two guards met him at the inside kitchen door.

They went down.

Two more appeared in the outside entrance. Dorn sent them back and off the porch.

Fast moving footfalls from a side hall leading into the main hall stopped when Dorn, fired two warning shots through the open entryway.

Gripping the handrail he pulled himself to the landing.

Standing above him was Forslund Nauman.

The pudgy fist held a luger. The single slug he got off imbedded itself in his father's portrait. Two cartridges left in the M-16. Dorn fired them.

Forsland fell on his back. The top half of the Nazi's head was pulp.

Wheezing, Dorn took his time advancing on the room where the respirator was.

Behind the closed door the respirator stopped.

A high-pitched alarm sounded.

Dorn went in.

A shriveled, toothless, bald man lay, unmoving, on cotton sheets. A wool blanket, gray as his skin, covered his feet. The sweat-ringed blue nightshirt extended to his ankles. Tubes in his pinched nose and pasty arms were connected to the machine next to the bed.

Waste tubes bunched the night shirt at its sides.

Emil Nauman's sunken cheeks turned black.

"Beat me before I beat you, bastard," Dorn said.

"Don't shit," Krager said behind Dorn. "Only me."

Eyes wild, Dorn stumbled, fell back into Krager's arms.

"Where you been?" Dorn said. "Diddling a fraulein?"

"Looking for a way out. I found it."

They crossed to the walk-in closet. The dark suits and storm trooper uniforms stank of moth balls and sweat.

A sliding door in the back wall was open. Krager thumbed a wall switch. A ceiling light went on.

At the bottom of the stairs a swing out door was ajar.

They went through it and into the solarium on the west side. A door to the outside was unlocked.

A few feet south was the west end of the open front porch. The van, a few feet away, was aimed at the incline to the gate and, beyond, Delaware Road.

Krager released the hand brake; the van coasted to the fence. At the open gate Krager gunned the motor and, a half mile from Ten Eleven Delaware Road, he said:

"Something odd about this whole arrangement."

Dorn woke up. "Huh?"

"When I heard the shots in back, I scattered with everyone else. I hid outside. The goose steppers took off toward the noise. The door to the closet where the guns were kept was open."

He flashed the three-fifty-seven under his jacket.

"I was about to go back outside through the front door when I heard people pounding at the door. I headed in, groping for another way out. I found the door leading upstairs. The solarium was full of uniforms and suits. Don't know who the suits were. I'm up the stairs halfway when more gunshots. Distantlike. The stairway was narrow. Like a coffin. My stink was making me sick but I kept climbing until I got the slider, into the closet. I thought the stink making me wheeze was the old uniforms. But it wasn't. The smell came from the bed and what was in it. I knew right then that the old Nazi was decaying, and a loud fart would send him all the way down. I was tempted to move the pillow from under his head to his nose and mouth. I decided to give you the pleasure. I waited there in the room shadows, waited for the excitement to quiet down. I was nearly ready to go down those stairs when you showed."

Dorn pursed his lips. "Strange how quiet the house got after Nauman passed. Like when he died they also did likewise."

"Yeah, that's what I meant. Strange, no?"

"Unless those suits . . ." He told Krager who they were. "Unless they rounded up the skinfreaks, got them out of there, waited for us to do the same."

"Why would they do that?"

"Why does the government do what it does?" Dorn said. "Tired of baby-sitting. Wet nursing. Pissed at the skinheads for complicating life. Pissed at the local law for bungling containment. But . . ." he shrugged. "I don't know."

Dorn told about his meeting with Forslund Nauman.

"Put the kay-bosh on the Naumans."

"In six months that rat palace will be a Nazi shrine."

Krager tapped the brake. "Not if there's nothing there."

"Take a howitzer and plenty of time to level it."

"One good one. With what I got in back. Up ahead's the U-turn.

"Take it."

XXXVII

THE GATE WAS OPEN.

One light in the downstairs hall; one upstairs.

The front door was open.

Kramer backed the van to the porch.

He put on the flame-resistant suit.

Dorn helped carry the explosives into the hall. Kramer carried a load upstairs, came down, placed another load in the hall under the stairs.

He beckoned, pointed.

Kramer hoisted the equipment. Dorn hauled the pepper-pungent explosives.

The light switch, on the kitchen wall, was next to the basement door.

Down the winding stairs into the box-shaped room. It smelled of humidity, the sewer drain, and wood crates.

Stacked against the wall, floor to ceiling, were boxes of imported wine.

"Liebfraumilch" imprinted on their sides.

"Mildred's drink. Fruit from the Rhine country," Dorn said.

"Drink's on the house." Pat found a short stack, broke open one of the crates, handed a bottle.

Dorn took it. "Thanks."

Krager placed the charge in the room's center. He arranged the leader wires. Unspooled the wires up the stairs, across the kitchen and hall floors, onto the porch, down the steps to the gravel between the bottom step and cobble stone path.

"Pick me up at the gate, Carl."

Dorn parked outside the gate.

He tore the seal, uncorked the bottle.

The smell that assailed his nostrils was unfamiliar.

He took the nub of a pencil from his jacket pocket. Stuck the nub in the liquid.

Looked at what was left of the pencil. He remembered.

"Crap!"

Krager uncoiled the last of the wire. The detonator hung like a useless limb. He was halfway down the drive, about forty feet.

He sat behind a sturdy oak tree beside the driveway.

He punched the detonator button.

The blast's force threw him back.

"Damn," he said. "It shouldn't be this strong."

The roar shook the van.

XXXVIII

THE FLASH SHATTERED the helmet's shield, undulated across Krager's irises. Heat sucked moisture and air.

A flaming ball squeezed through the front door, surged across the entryway, incinerating trees, consuming the lawn, rolled toward Krager.

He couldn't see it coming but he felt it.

On his feet he charged toward the gate, slipping, falling on his belly, rolling away from the surging inferno.

Dorn saw it coming.

As it engaged the trees it increased strength.

In the distance, dogs howled.

A distant siren counterpointed the sound of cannons firing.

A black wall of smoke fell around Krager.

The back-flash engulfed him. Hot tongues licked the suit, seeking an opening.

Wind came up, passing over the castle, swooped down to slap the back-flash, propel it and its creator closer to the gate.

Dorn tromped the accelerator.

Hitting potholes, throwing clustered leaves, the van swiveled like a street hooker parading the merchandise.

The vehicle bounced down a two-lane road for a mile, outdistancing what chased him.

The hell fire carried Krager to the iron fence, slammed him against it, dropped him there. He stood, fell, clawed at the blackened vegetation.

Brown clumps filled his hands. When he squeezed, they disintegrated.

He fell against the fence.

"Where are you, Carl?"

After a few seconds, he didn't care.

XXXVIX

TWO DAYS LATER, when the eleven alarm inferno had exhausted itself, the Nauman compound was ash. Seventy surrounding acres and their manor houses were gone. Retired bank vice presidents, former mayors of midwest cities, drug kingpins huddled around vans that dispensed, at no charge, clothing, bedding and hot meals.

News reports claimed that a ruptured gas main had ignited.

The regional utility denied this.

Special Agent in charge William Sowers held a news conference in the town square, within sight of the bus depot.

"For the last forty years the FBI has protected Emil Nauman, a longtime Withersville resident and a retired physicist who, as you may know, helped greatly in this country's race to perfect a number of weapons, used with great success by the United States against her enemies. For his contributions Dr. Nauman and his family were given the same protection afforded retired presidents and their families. However it became known only recently that Emil Nauman and his son were engaged in activities detrimental to this country's security. The president and his advisors have, for many weeks, conducted discussions with members of the House and Senate on the proper course of action, regarding Dr. Nauman's recent activities. As many of you know, over the last several years, the number of neo-Nazi hate groups within our borders has grown. U.S. citizens who have contributed to the enrichment of our democratic way of life have been victimized by those seeking to destroy what this country stands for.

To quote our president: "We won't stand for it."

"Before any determinations were made concerning a suitable response to the charges from unidentified sources that the Naumans were indeed engaged in crimes that, if not stopped, would result in anarchy . . ."

He sipped water and a shot of Canadian Club.

"Before a course of action was determined, persons unknown raided the Nauman compound on Delaware Road two days ago, detonating explosives stored in the Nauman basement. Blame has been placed with a upstart group of neo-Nazis headed by a young woman from the midwest. As of this date she and members of the group have not been located. The investigation is on-going. Meantime, a number of Nauman's group were captured. Their interrogations continue in a mid-eastern country.

"You can be assured the FBI will find and deal with these subversives. Our agency will report further when developments warrant. Thank you and good afternoon."

He ignored the reporters.

Waddling toward a black limo he said to the agent at his side:

"Got an extra hemorrhoid suppository you can spare?"

XL

A T SIX THAT NIGHT Dorn drank hot tea with lemon at the Withersville bus depot coffee shop. He had the counter to himself. Not even the homeless, passing through Idaho, sat near this unshaven, urine and sweat-stinking old man.

He ordered a sandwich.

The counterman shook his head, pointed at the door.

Dorn showed his credit card and state employees ID.

The counterman reached under the counter, brought out a baseball bat.

Outside, Dorn waited for the anger to pass. South winds blew away the smoke and ash, the stench of charred wood.

Then he started toward the depot lot and the van.

The black limo stopped in front of him. The back door opened. William Sowers beckoned.

"Thought it was you. Get in."

Dorn tightened the seat belt.

He was told: "Been looking for you and the torch since Hell broke out on Delaware Road."

"I've been busy."

"What doing?"

"Resting."

"Not at the Motor Inn."

"Camped out."

"Hoped you were still in town."

"Nice to be missed."

"Had dinner?"

"Hot tea."

"Clean you up. Then have another. With a side of ham and eggs."

The limo parked in front of the Motor Inn. After a bladder draining, shave and shower and an underwear change, he put on a crisp, clear light blue shirt bought en route to the motel.

A long look at the bed before he returned to the limo.

Sowers capped the flask. "I'd offer you a jolt, only less for you, more for me."

"Your breath is jolt enough."

The driver and agent up front laughed.

The restaurant Sowers chose was the Taverna, a Greek place on a hill. Sentry lights and the subdued lights of the nearby manor houses and a glimpse of someone inside passing an undraped window, and a jogger with a dog on a leash were the only signs of life.

Below and north there was a dark gap where Delaware Road had been.

Sowers ordered a New York Strip steak with Greek potatoes, salad with olives and feta cheese, green beans and a demitasse of strong Greek coffee.

"How's the Greek oatmeal?" Dorn said.

The waiter said: "The Greek gyro plate is better."

"Greek oatmeal's fine."

"Don't know what that is. But we will try. What to drink?"

"How's the Greek tea?"

"Lipton's."

The waiter departed.

Sowers poured a Canadian Club splash down his throat. "Yes, sir. There is a God."

"Really love that stuff."

"Like the nun in the laundry room said: We have our habits."

He draped his jacket over the chair back. The white shirt's light blue vertical stripes were obliterated by sweat. Silver cuff links anchored the cuffs to his thick wrists.

"Best part of my day is when it's done, and I'm in my robe and slippers with a tall taste of Heaven in my fat grip and the voice mail picks up my calls and I got a fire going behind the grate. When's your favorite time?"

"Every minute of every day."

The coffee and tea arrived. "Keep the coffee coming," Sowers said.

In a corner two waiters chatted. The bartender polished a glass.

Sowers said: "Beating the evening rush is how I like it. gives us a chance to discuss the week's events."

"Dodging questions is how I like it."

"Not too many, then. Can't have you dodging yourself into a stroke." He drank the coffee in a single swallow. Wiping his mouth, he said; "What happened on Delaware Road? Take your time."

"Not much of that left."

"We gave you the chance to get out."

"Shot our way out."

"You and the torch."

"Yes."

"Where is he?"

"Gone to glory."

"We were on to your partner, the firefly. He freelanced for the Naumans. Know that?"

Dorn nodded.

"Left a trail of burned out religious houses from Iowa to here."

"Heard that."

"We heard he and you were headed this way. Hoped you would put the old man down."

"When I found him he was dead."

"Can't prove that. Where's the torch?"

"In fragments out there on Delaware Road."

"Got caught in his own inferno."

"In Nauman's basement there were wine bottles. What came out of the vineyard were the labels. The bottles were filled with high octane. I found out when I uncorked a bottle. He never did find out."

"Why didn't you leave?"

"Planned to. Too weary to make the jump right then. I pulled onto a clear space off the highway for a short nap. It lasted two days."

"When this broad phoned in your plans we decided to let you help us. You see, Mr. Dorn, funding for the Nazi's round-the-clock took money from other projects."

The meal arrived.

Sowers had a brandy snifter for dessert.

They sat on a curbside bench in front of the restaurant. Dorn smoked.

"Tobacco's lethal," Sowers said. "Never smoked."

"If one habit doesn't kill you, another will."

"Drop you at the bus station or the motel?"

"Depot's fine."

Sowers nipped at the flask. "My report'll go easy on you."

"Doesn't matter. I'm waiting. I can wait at home or in prison."

Dorn yawned.

"Up to driving?"

"Asleep, I could drive."

"Drop you at the motel. Pick you up after you've had a good rest. Drive you to the bus station. No charge."

"If I can't make it to the motel, I will park it."

Bowers stood. "Bus station then."

XLI

DORN DROVE the van to the motel. He checked out, headed for the Withersville city limits.

At the interstate, they were on him.

Eight P.M.

Over the road transports passed in their inside lanes.

He got in the outside lane, heading out of town. The cruise control was set at fifty.

The limo stayed fifty feet behind.

"Fat bastard." With one hand he loaded the rocket launcher, propped it on the passenger's seat.

"Think I wouldn't catch on? Telling me all that crap? Waiting now to hit a secluded patch before the cannons come out? Before this is over you'll be flame-dancing. My homage to a dear friend, a partner in the evil that rids the world of a greater evil."

On the northbound curve he speeded up, was around the curve and into a tangle of trees.

The limo passed, stopped and U-turned a mile down the highway, and returned. Dorn had the rocket launcher balanced on the hood, aimed at the limo.

The front doors opened. The overhead light showed two men getting out.

Dorn touched the trigger.

Forty-four caliber handguns at hip level, they advanced on the van.

Dorn sent the missile to their left, into the limo.

The impact rattled his teeth. The flash turned the trees red. While debris cascaded around him, the light turned gray.

The limo was a misshapen ball.

The pair on the blackened ground were smoldering flesh and bone.

Dorn drove around the embers.

Dawn before the next rest stop. A day's rest.

"Then I'm coming for you, Sowers, you government issue boozer."

His prostate twinged.

He thought about Mildred.

The pain went away.

RAMBLE HOUSE's

HARRY STEPHEN KEELER WEBWORK MYSTERIES

(RH) indicates the title is available ONLY in the RAMBLE HOUSE edition

Keeler Related Works

A To Izzard: A Harry Stephen Keeler Companion by Fender Tucker — Articles and stories about Harry, by Harry, and in his style. Included is a compleat bibliography.

Wild About Harry: Reviews of Keeler Novels — Edited by Richard Polt & Fender Tucker — 22 reviews of works by Harry Stephen Keeler from *Keeler News*. A perfect introduction to the author.

The Keeler Keyhole Collection: Annotated newsletter rants from Harry Stephen Keeler, edited by Francis M. Nevins. Over 400 pages of incredibly personal Keeleriana.

Fakealoo — Pastiches of the style of Harry Stephen Keeler by selected demented members of the HSK Society. Updated every year with the new winner.

RAMBLE HOUSE's OTHER LOONS

Strands of the Web: Short Stories of Harry Stephen Keeler — Edited and Introduced by Fred Cleaver

The Sam McCain Novels — Ed Gorman's terrific series includes *The Day the Music Died, Wake Up Little Susie* and *Will You Still Love Me Tomorrow?*

A Shot Rang Out — Three decades of reviews from Jon Breen

Blood Moon — The first of the Robert Payne series by Ed Gorman

The Time Armada — Fox B. Holden's 1953 SF gem.

Black River Falls — Suspense from the master, Ed Gorman

Sideslip — 1968 SF masterpiece by Ted White and Dave Van Arnam

The Triune Man — Mindscrambling science fiction from Richard A. Lupoff

Detective Duff Unravels It — Episodic mysteries by Harvey O'Higgins

Mysterious Martin, the Master of Murder — Two versions of a strange 1912 novel by Tod Robbins about a man who writes books that can kill.

The Master of Mysteries — 1912 novel of supernatural sleuthing by Gelett Burgess

Dago Red — 22 tales of dark suspense by Bill Pronzini

The Night Remembers — A 1991 Jack Walsh mystery from Ed Gorman

Rough Cut & New, Improved Murder — Ed Gorman's first two novels

Hollywood Dreams — A novel of the Depression by Richard O'Brien

Six Gelett Burgess Novels — *The Master of Mysteries, The White Cat, Two O'Clock Courage, Ladies in Boxes, Find the Woman, The Heart Line*

The Organ Reader — A huge compilation of just about everything published in the 1971-1972 radical bay-area newspaper, *THE ORGAN*.

A Clear Path to Cross — Sharon Knowles short mystery stories by Ed Lynskey

Old Times' Sake — Short stories by James Reasoner from Mike Shayne Magazine

Freaks and Fantasies — Eerie tales by Tod Robbins, collaborator of Tod Browning on the film FREAKS.

Five Jim Harmon Sleaze Double Novels — *Vixen Hollow/Celluloid Scandal, The Man Who Made Maniacs/Silent Siren, Ape Rape/Wanton Witch, Sex Burns Like Fire/Twist Session*, and *Sudden Lust/Passion Strip*. More doubles to come!

Marblehead: A Novel of H.P. Lovecraft — A long-lost masterpiece from Richard A. Lupoff. Published for the first time!

The Compleat Ova Hamlet — Parodies of SF authors by Richard A. Lupoff – New edition!

The Secret Adventures of Sherlock Holmes — Three Sherlockian pastiches by the Brooklyn author/publisher, Gary Lovisi.

The Universal Holmes — Richard A. Lupoff's 2007 collection of five Holmesian pastiches and a recipe for giant rat stew.

Four Joel Townsley Rogers Novels — By the author of *The Red Right Hand: Once In a Red Moon, Lady With the Dice, The Stopped Clock, Never Leave My Bed*

Two Joel Townsley Rogers Story Collections — Night of Horror and Killing Time

Twenty Norman Berrow Novels — *The Bishop's Sword, Ghost House, Don't Go Out After Dark, Claws of the Cougar, The Smokers of Hashish, The Secret Dancer, Don't Jump Mr. Boland!, The Footprints of Satan, Fingers for Ransom, The Three Tiers of Fantasy, The Spaniard's Thumb, The Eleventh Plague, Words Have Wings, One Thrilling Night, The Lady's in Danger, It Howls at Night, The Terror in the Fog, Oil Under the Window, Murder in the Melody, The Singing Room*

The N. R. De Mexico Novels — Robert Bragg presents *Marijuana Girl, Madman on a Drum, Private Chauffeur* in one volume.

Four Chelsea Quinn Yarbro Novels featuring Charlie Moon — *Ogilvie, Tallant and Moon, Music When the Sweet Voice Dies, Poisonous Fruit* and *Dead Mice*

Four Walter S. Masterman Mysteries — *The Green Toad, The Flying Beast, The Yellow Mistletoe* and *The Wrong Verdict*, fantastic impossible plots. More to come.

Two Hake Talbot Novels — *Rim of the Pit, The Hangman's Handyman*. Classic locked room mysteries.

Two Alexander Laing Novels — *The Motives of Nicholas Holtz* and *Dr. Scarlett*, stories of medical mayhem and intrigue from the 30s.

Four David Hume Novels — *Corpses Never Argue, Cemetery First Stop, Make Way for the Mourners, Eternity Here I Come*, and more to come.

Three Wade Wright Novels — *Echo of Fear, Death At Nostalgia Street* and *It Leads to Murder*, with more to come!

Six Rupert Penny Novels — *Policeman's Holiday, Policeman's Evidence, Lucky Policeman, Policeman in Armour, Sealed Room Murder, Sweet Poison*, classic mysteries.

Five Jack Mann Novels — Strange murder in the English countryside. *Gees' First Case, Nightmare Farm, Grey Shapes, The Ninth Life, The Glass Too Many.*

Seven Max Afford Novels — *Owl of Darkness, Death's Mannikins, Blood on His Hands, The Dead Are Blind, The Sheep and the Wolves, Sinners in Paradise* and *Two Locked Room Mysteries and a Ripping Yarn* by one of Australia's finest novelists.

Five Joseph Shallit Novels — *The Case of the Billion Dollar Body, Lady Don't Die on My Doorstep, Kiss the Killer, Yell Bloody Murder, Take Your Last Look.* One of America's best 50's authors.

Two Crimson Clown Novels — By Johnston McCulley, author of the Zorro novels, *The Crimson Clown* and *The Crimson Clown Again.*

The Best of 10-Story Book — edited by Chris Mikul, over 35 stories from the literary magazine Harry Stephen Keeler edited.

A Young Man's Heart — A forgotten early classic by Cornell Woolrich

The Anthony Boucher Chronicles — edited by Francis M. Nevins
Book reviews by Anthony Boucher written for the *San Francisco Chronicle,* 1942 – 1947. Essential and fascinating reading.

Muddled Mind: Complete Works of Ed Wood, Jr. — David Hayes and Hayden Davis deconstruct the life and works of a mad genius.

Gadsby — A lipogram (a novel without the letter E). Ernest Vincent Wright's last work, published in 1939 right before his death.

My First Time: The One Experience You Never Forget — Michael Birchwood — 64 true first-person narratives of how they lost it.

Automaton — Brilliant treatise on robotics: 1928-style! By H. Stafford Hatfield

The Incredible Adventures of Rowland Hern — Rousing 1928 impossible crimes by Nicholas Olde.

Slammer Days — Two full-length prison memoirs: *Men into Beasts* (1952) by George Sylvester Viereck and *Home Away From Home* (1962) by Jack Woodford

Murder in Black and White — 1931 classic tennis whodunit by Evelyn Elder

Killer's Caress — Cary Moran's 1936 hardboiled thriller

The Golden Dagger — 1951 Scotland Yard yarn by E. R. Punshon

Beat Books #1 — Two beatnik classics, *A Sea of Thighs* by Ray Kainen and *Village Hipster* by J.X. Williams

A Smell of Smoke — 1951 English countryside thriller by Miles Burton

Ruled By Radio — 1925 futuristic novel by Robert L. Hadfield & Frank E. Farncombe

Murder in Silk — A 1937 Yellow Peril novel of the silk trade by Ralph Trevor

The Case of the Withered Hand — 1936 potboiler by John G. Brandon

Finger-prints Never Lie — A 1939 classic detective novel by John G. Brandon

Inclination to Murder — 1966 thriller by New Zealand's Harriet Hunter

Invaders from the Dark — Classic werewolf tale from Greye La Spina

Fatal Accident — Murder by automobile, a 1936 mystery by Cecil M. Wills

The Devil Drives — A prison and lost treasure novel by Virgil Markham

Dr. Odin — Douglas Newton's 1933 potboiler comes back to life.

The Chinese Jar Mystery — Murder in the manor by John Stephen Strange, 1934

The Julius Caesar Murder Case — A classic 1935 re-telling of the assassination by Wallace Irwin that's much more fun than the Shakespeare version

West Texas War and Other Western Stories — by Gary Lovisi

The Contested Earth and Other SF Stories — A never-before published space opera and seven short stories by Jim Harmon.

Tales of the Macabre and Ordinary — Modern twisted horror by Chris Mikul, author of the *Bizarrism* series.

The Gold Star Line — Seaboard adventure from L.T. Reade and Robert Eustace.

The Werewolf vs the Vampire Woman — Hard to believe ultraviolence by either Arthur M. Scarm or Arthur M. Scram.

Black Hogan Strikes Again — Australia's Peter Renwick pens a tale of the outback.

Don Diablo: Book of a Lost Film — Two-volume treatment of a western by Paul Landres, with diagrams. Intro by Francis M. Nevins.

The Charlie Chaplin Murder Mystery — Movie hijinks by Wes D. Gehring

The Koky Comics — A collection of all of the 1978-1981 Sunday and daily comic strips by Richard O'Brien and Mort Gerberg, in two volumes.

Suzy — Another collection of comic strips from Richard O'Brien and Bob Vojtko

Dime Novels: Ramble House's 10-Cent Books — *Knife in the Dark* by Robert Leslie Bellem, *Hot Lead* and *Song of Death* by Ed Earl Repp, *A Hashish House in New York* by H.H. Kane, and five more.

Blood in a Snap — The *Finnegan's Wake* of the 21st century, by Jim Weiler and Al Gorithm

Stakeout on Millennium Drive — Award-winning Indianapolis Noir — Ian Woollen.

Dope Tales #1 — Two dope-riddled classics; *Dope Runners* by Gerald Grantham and *Death Takes the Joystick* by Phillip Condé.

Dope Tales #2 — Two more narco-classics; *The Invisible Hand* by Rex Dark and *The Smokers of Hashish* by Norman Berrow.

Dope Tales #3 — Two enchanting novels of opium by the master, Sax Rohmer. *Dope* and *The Yellow Claw*.

Tenebrae — Ernest G. Henham's 1898 horror tale brought back.

The Singular Problem of the Stygian House-Boat — Two classic tales by John Kendrick Bangs about the denizens of Hades.

Tiresias — Psychotic modern horror novel by Jonathan M. Sweet.

The One After Snelling — Kickass modern noir from Richard O'Brien.

The Sign of the Scorpion — 1935 Edmund Snell tale of oriental evil.

The House of the Vampire — 1907 poetic thriller by George S. Viereck.

An Angel in the Street — Modern hardboiled noir by Peter Genovese.

The Devil's Mistress — Scottish gothic tale by J. W. Brodie-Innes.

The Lord of Terror — 1925 mystery with master-criminal, Fantômas.

The Lady of the Terraces — 1925 adventure by E. Charles Vivian.

My Deadly Angel — 1955 Cold War drama by John Chelton.

Prose Bowl — Futuristic satire — Bill Pronzini & Barry N. Malzberg .

Satan's Den Exposed — True crime in Truth or Consequences New Mexico — Award-winning journalism by the *Desert Journal*.

The Amorous Intrigues & Adventures of Aaron Burr — by Anonymous — Hot historical action.

I Stole $16,000,000 — A true story by cracksman Herbert E. Wilson.

The Black Dark Murders — Vintage 50s college murder yarn by Milt Ozaki, writing as Robert O. Saber.

Sex Slave — Potboiler of lust in the days of Cleopatra — Dion Leclerq.

You'll Die Laughing — Bruce Elliott's 1945 novel of murder at a practical joker's English countryside manor.

The Private Journal & Diary of John H. Surratt — The memoirs of the man who conspired to assassinate President Lincoln.

Dead Man Talks Too Much — Hollywood boozer by Weed Dickenson.

Red Light — History of legal prostitution in Shreveport Louisiana by Eric Brock. Includes wonderful photos of the houses and the ladies.

A Snark Selection — Lewis Carroll's *The Hunting of the Snark* with two Snarkian chapters by Harry Stephen Keeler — Illustrated by Gavin L. O'Keefe.

Ripped from the Headlines! — The Jack the Ripper story as told in the newspaper articles in the *New York* and *London Times*.

Geronimo — S. M. Barrett's 1905 autobiography of a noble American.

The White Peril in the Far East — Sidney Lewis Gulick's 1905 indictment of the West and assurance that Japan would never attack the U.S.

The Compleat Calhoon — All of Fender Tucker's works: Includes *The Totah Trilogy*, *Weed, Women and Song* and *Tales from the Tower*, plus a CD of all of his songs.

RAMBLE HOUSE
Fender Tucker, Prop.
www.ramblehouse.com   fender@ramblehouse.com
228-826-1783   10329 Sheephead Drive, Vancleave MS 39565

www.ingramcontent.com/pod-product-compliance
Lightning Source LLC
Chambersburg PA
CBHW020701030726
47498CB00002B/596